"The abductors are still out there."

Nicole took her gaze off the road for a moment to peer at Jack, struck by the sorrow she heard in his voice. She remembered him saying his sister had died and wondered if there was a connection there. About to open her mouth to ask, she froze, arrested as Jack's expression twisted in horror.

"Look out!" He reached over and jerked the wheel to the right. She whipped her head around in time to see a crop-dusting plane headed in their direction, nearly on top of them.

"Why is he flying over the road!" Nicole spun the wheel, sending the cruiser off the road and skidding into the grass while the plane passed them. She hit the gas and her tires spun in the grass and mud before finding traction again on the paved road.

Her questions were answered when the plane did a staggering loop in the air and roared back toward them. She floored it, trying to outrun this new threat. Bullets rained down on the road from the craft.

They'd become the killer's new target.

Dana R. Lynn grew up in Illinois. She met her husband at a wedding and told her parents she'd met the man she was going to marry. Nineteen months later, they were married. Today, they live in rural Pennsylvania with their three children and a variety of animals. In addition to writing, she works as a teacher for the deaf and hard of hearing and is active in her church.

Books by Dana R. Lynn

Love Inspired Suspense

Amish Country Justice

Plain Target
Plain Retribution
Amish Christmas Abduction
Amish Country Ambush
Amish Christmas Emergency
Guarding the Amish Midwife
Hidden in Amish Country
Plain Refuge
Deadly Amish Reunion
Amish Country Threats
Covert Amish Investigation
Amish Christmas Escape
Amish Cradle Conspiracy

Visit the Author Profile page at LoveInspired.com for more titles.

AMISH CRADLE CONSPIRACY

DANA R. LYNN

LOVE INSPIRED SUSPENSE
INSPIRATIONAL ROMANCE

LOVE INSPIRED® SUSPENSE
INSPIRATIONAL ROMANCE

ISBN-13: 978-1-335-55505-2

Recycling programs for this product may not exist in your area.

Amish Cradle Conspiracy

For questions and comments about the quality of this book, please contact us at CustomerService@Harlequin.com.

Love Inspired
22 Adelaide St. West, 41st Floor
Toronto, Ontario M5H 4E3, Canada
www.LoveInspired.com

Printed in U.S.A.

He hath shewed thee, O man, what is good;
and what doth the Lord require of thee, but to do justly,
and to love mercy, and to walk humbly with thy God?
—*Micah* 6:8

To the first responders who put themselves at risk
in order to serve others. God bless you
for your service and dedication.

ONE

Sergeant Nicole Dawson glanced at the dashboard when the phone rang. Seeing her boss's name and number glowing back at her, she punched the button. She rode shotgun while her partner, Sergeant Kathy Bartlett, sat behind the wheel, taking each curve on the twisting Ohio back road with white-knuckled concentration, her lips pinched together.

Kathy hated driving fast. Nicole definitely didn't want her looking away from the road ahead of them. As Kathy steered around another corner, Nicole reached out and braced herself on the smooth dash in front of her.

"Hi Chief. This is Sergeant Dawson."

"Sergeant, what's your ETA?" Police chief Mike Spencer's voice boomed through the car's speakers. He had one of those voices that rumbled and carried, no matter how quiet he attempted to talk. It reminded her of a human thunderstorm, even though the man himself was one of the calmest people she'd ever met.

Nicole leaned over, angling her head to glance at the GPS on the dashboard of the Sutter Springs Police Department cruiser, where the map was displayed.

"Four minutes, Chief." Nicole tapped her fingers on

her thigh, trying to control her nervous energy. Lives were at stake. Every second counted. If she'd been driving, they would have been going at least eight miles an hour faster. It would only have knocked off a few seconds, but even a second or two could be crucial.

They had already been in Kathy's car when the call came through around eight that morning. Otherwise, she would have taken the wheel herself.

"I have backup headed your way. Hansen and Zilhaver should be there in under ten. If possible, wait to enter the building. I don't want any carelessness. Or any casualties."

Hansen was still a rookie, but Zilhaver had some experience behind him. He was just shy of his sergeant stripes.

"That might not be possible, Chief." Nicole mentally replayed the phone call she'd received less than an hour ago. "The woman who saw our missing person said she was wounded. And she thought she saw a gun on one of the men she was with. Lucy Hilty is eight months pregnant. And Leah's less than two years old."

They'd been combing the streets for Lucy, an Amish woman from one of the local districts, ever since the woman's family had reported her and her youngest child missing two days earlier. Nicole knew the area and its people well from previous assignments. Although she didn't see her often, she'd interacted with Lucy previously and had seen her daughter.

"I'm aware of that, Sergeant." The chief paused. "Any word on her child?"

"No." Nicole swallowed past the fear the word brought. Nicole had nearly worn out her knees praying for the safe return of both mother and her young daughter. It terrified her that the caller hadn't seen Leah with Lucy.

A sigh drifted through the phone. They all knew that the longer a victim remained missing, the less likely they would be found alive. "Be cautious. Don't take any unnecessary risks."

"Understood." Nicole disconnected the call. She hated the phrase "unnecessary risk." Three lives were in jeopardy. Leah, Lucy and the unborn child. Risks were part and parcel with wearing the badge, as far as she was concerned. That didn't make them any easier, though, when faced with life's horror stories.

They were only a minute out and were still running hot. Nicole frowned. They needed to be discreet, if they could manage it.

"Kath, let's kill the lights and the siren."

"Yeah." Kathy switched them off. "It wouldn't do to warn them we're coming."

Nicole frowned at the road ahead of them. All she saw was tall grass, lush from an abundance of rain, mud puddles and a long country road.

"Are you sure this is the right road?" Kathy peered into her rearview mirror.

"I think so. I've never been on it before."

"Me, neither. I just can't figure what kind of abandoned building would be back here. I mean, who builds a business on a dirt road?"

"We don't know it was a business." The woman on the phone hadn't said what kind of building it was. Only that it looked abandoned. She was from out of state and had been on the road by accident. The caller had said she'd seen the woman and two men entering an abandoned building and had given the address.

"There's a lot we don't know. I don't like it." Kathy flexed her fingers on the steering wheel.

Nicole shrugged. She'd plugged the address into the GPS, having never heard of the road, despite living in Sutter Springs for the past ten years and knowing the community well.

She'd liked Berlin County, Ohio, immediately. It was a welcome change from the hustle and bustle of Pittsburgh, Pennsylvania, where she'd grown up. Plus, it allowed her to distance herself from all those who knew of her father's duplicity and how it had destroyed her mother's life. She liked it well enough that she'd stayed, even after a brutal betrayal by her then fiancé, Jack, which had ended their relationship. Infidelity was the one thing she couldn't forgive or forget. She'd seen what her mother had suffered. That would never be her. Jack had denied it, but when she'd asked for more information, he'd also closed up, saying it was classified. How could she trust a man who wouldn't talk to her about something that important? She couldn't, and that was a truth she'd learned to live with.

Never again would she fall into that trap. On those infrequent times when she and Jack were together, she was polite and professional. Nothing more. Fortunately, he was no longer with the police department, having accepted a position with the FBI several years ago.

"Turn right at the next intersection." The robotic GPS voice pulled her back to the present. Kathy slowed, then braked at a stop sign almost completely hidden in the overgrown brush.

"That's an accident waiting to happen. Remind me to report it."

"Okay." Nicole straightened in her seat. At least they

were back on a paved surface. Half a mile down the road they reached their destination. A two-story build-ing with faux log cabin siding loomed before them. It had obviously been a house at one time.

Both women exited the vehicle, hands on their ser-vice weapons. The structure had seen better times. Shingles littered the ground surrounding the building. Large cobwebs clung from the faded sign in front, shiv-ering as if alive when a breeze stirred them.

Sunshine Day Care. Rather ironic if the perps were using the former day care to hide abducted children.

Hopefully, they wouldn't find any bodies. She read-justed her grip on the weapon.

There was no sign of movement, nor were there any other cars or vehicles in view. The hope she'd held that they might find Leah and Lucy began to fade.

Kathy motioned for Nicole to go around the right. Nodding, Nicole headed to the side. Near the back of the house, she halted. An older model compact car was parked near the back door. The vehicle the caller had seen. They were here.

Keeping low to avoid being spotted out the windows, she made her way back to the front. At the corner of the house, she paused, scanning the area for any vis-ible threats or signs of danger. All she saw was Kathy creeping back to the car. Nicole ducked down and ran to meet Kathy near the cruiser. She leaned one hip against the passenger door, keeping both hands on her weapon, holding it low and away from them.

"They're here." She jerked her head toward the side of the building. "I saw the car."

Kathy frowned, the lines around her mouth deepening, and squinted through the morning May sunlight to the door. "Backup should arrive at any—"

A shot rang out. Kathy yelled and dropped her Glock, grabbing her shoulder. The bullet had gone in right where her Kevlar vest ended.

Nicole shoved her partner down behind the cruiser and worked to remove the vest, hands shaking. A stain was already beginning to spread on her dark blue uniform shirt. Nicole squelched down the fear that clawed inside her. Kathy needed help now. Praying the bullet hadn't nicked the thoracoacromial artery, she crouched down and twisted to scan the area for danger. The hairs on the back of her neck raised. Lifting her head, she focused on the window above the front porch.

And stared into the face of a killer. It was hard to see clearly from that distance. She had a vague impression of a long face. Shaggy hair. There was something uneven about his features, but the window seemed to be warped. From where she stood, squinting at him, he was hazy. She couldn't see much at all.

She raised her weapon to get a shot off, but he was gone before she could shout "Police," let alone pull the trigger.

Could she identify him if she saw him again? It was doubtful. She hadn't gotten more than a vague idea of what he looked like. At least, she thought it was a man, based on the way he stood and the width of his shoulders.

Kathy groaned. Nicole lowered the weapon but kept it close by. She had to tend to her fallen partner. Peering into the other woman's face, Nicole pressed her lips together. Kathy's usually clear gaze was off. Her pupils seemed larger than normal. Not a good sign.

Gently pushing Kathy against the car, she opened the door and grabbed her coat from the floor. She needed something to stop the flow of blood. Kathy gasped when she pressed the material against her wound but made no other sound.

Using the radio attached to her shoulder, Nicole called dispatch and requested an ambulance for an officer down at the scene. Kathy frowned, but Nicole ignored her partner, intent on getting help ASAP. Kathy was losing blood at an alarming rate.

"I'm dispatching an ambulance now, Sergeant," the voice on the other end of the radio assured her. She bit her lip so she wouldn't tell her to make them hurry.

Nicole was never good at waiting.

The window above her head shattered. Another shot. She kept the door open so it could act as a shield. Daring to peek above the rim, she attempted to get a better look at the sniper but couldn't see anyone this time. Given the angle of the shot, she wasn't even positive he was shooting from the same place.

"Where's my backup?" she demanded into her radio.

"They should be pulling in any second. Hang on." She heard the dispatcher talking to another driver.

"Tell them to hang back out of range. The shooter is inside the house. No sign of another gunman."

A third shot hit the ground next to the door. What if a shot slipped by and hit them from under the door? They needed to move behind the cruiser. It took some maneuvering to scoot to the back of the vehicle without standing, carrying her partner with her. Kathy's breathing had gained a rasp Nicole didn't like. Kathy couldn't hold the coat to her own wound, which meant

Nicole had to stay with her and couldn't fire her weapon back at the sniper.

"Go. I'll wait here."

Nicole didn't like the breathless quality of Kathy's voice, so unlike her normal robust tones.

"Help should be here soon. I'll wait." She kept her voice calm, even though her level of anxiety was increasing by the second. Kathy's skin was pale and waxy, and her eyes were growing hazy. Shock. Her partner needed emergency care.

"Hold on, Kathy. They're on their way. Soon." Even while she talked, Nicole wrapped her arms around her partner and lowered her carefully to the ground before checking her wound. It was still bleeding, so she continued to press firmly.

Less than a minute later, wheels hit the gravel behind them. Nicole glanced over her shoulder, her right-hand tightening on her Glock and her left remaining on Kathy's shoulder. A blue-and-white ambulance parked behind them. The doors swung open, and two paramedics swooped out of the vehicle.

"Keep low!" Nicole watched them come closer, both crouched as they hurried.

A police cruiser pulled in behind the ambulance. The doors opened and two Sutter Springs police officers and one FBI agent spilled out. Her gaze glossed over the officers and settled on the special agent dressed in a sports jacket and tie stepping into view. His blue-green eyes locked on Nicole and her stomach bottomed out.

Jack.

Nicole was safe. He scanned her injuries. His pulse sped up when he saw the blood splattered on her neck, arms and hands. It wasn't hers, he realized quickly. His concern shifted to the officer on the ground, a sergeant by the three yellow stripes on her uniform shirt, an exact replica of Nicole's.

The moment he'd learned who was at the scene, he'd felt like an iron fist had reached into his chest and grabbed his heart. They'd been in love once, before he'd signed on with the FBI. And taken on the case that had forced him to hide the truth from her.

It had broken something inside him to allow her to believe he'd cheated on her, but his hands had been tied. He'd been on an undercover mission during the last few months at the police department, working with the FBI. He wasn't allowed to discuss the details.

Then his personal life had imploded. First Nicole had broken up with him and shattered his heart. Then anger had taken over. She should have known him better, trusted him more when he'd told her it was classified information. But she hadn't. At the first sign of gossip, she'd bailed, tossed his ring in his face and stopped talking to him.

Angry, he'd given up trying to explain. When he'd packed up his apartment and moved to Columbus, he didn't bother to say goodbye, knowing they were done.

He was still grieving the loss of Nicole when his sister had been murdered and he'd become an instant father. His niece, Chloe, was his joy now. Making sure those involved with his sister's demise paid had become his focus. One day, Chloe would ask him what happened to her mother's killer, and he wanted to have an answer for her.

Jack took a deep breath, then focused on scanning the scene before him. The paramedics were already taking charge of the injured officer, who was showing signs of shock.

"We'll cover you while you get her into the ambulance," Nicole said. She and the other officers got their guns ready. Jack joined them. Nicole hadn't looked at him since he arrived, but that didn't matter. He was here to do a job, and somewhere in the house, someone with a gun had already taken out one officer. He forced his mind away from Nicole, standing just a few feet from him, and continued to get his bearings. The shattered window he'd already noted.

Behind them, the ambulance doors slammed. He relaxed slightly when the emergency vehicle made its exit without incident.

"Have any shots been fired in the past few minutes?" He made eye contact with Nicole. She stared back like he was a stranger instead of the man she'd once planned to marry.

"No. That doesn't mean the threat is gone."

"Obviously." He frowned, thinking. Before he could continue, Nicole took over. She was the senior officer on-site. The FBI was working in conjunction with the police department, but at the moment, the police department had jurisdiction.

"Okay, listen up. They know we're here. A pregnant woman and her child have been abducted. The woman, Lucy Hilty, has been spotted, her child has not. She may be injured. An eyewitness claimed that she thought that was the case. Either way, we need to breach the building. It's unclear how many guns are at play."

Efficiently, she laid out the plan. Cautiously, the group approached the former day care. It looked like it could have been a house at one time, long ago. The door was unlocked. When she opened it, Jack held his breath, his muscles tight, ready to spring in front of her at any moment.

Nothing.

They had taken two steps into the structure when a male voice shouted at the end of the hall. The officers paused. A woman screamed from a room near the back. Nicole sucked in a quiet breath but didn't say anything. A second later, footsteps thumped out the back door.

One set of steps. There were at least two people in the house, probably more.

Nicole waved at the officers to follow the steps. They slipped past her and Jack.

Jack tilted his head. Scuffling noises reached his ears. Someone was wrestling. He pointed in the direction of the sounds, urgency pounding in his blood. She nodded and they flattened themselves against the wall and made their way toward the noises. He kept his weapon pointed to the floor. The last thing he wanted was to shoot Nicole in the back if something jumped out at them. She held hers aloft. It made his skin itch, knowing she was going in first. But he didn't have the right or the authority to take the lead.

A car revved and tires spun outside. Someone was getting away. There was a shout near the back of the house. Footsteps pounded outside a minute later and then two car doors slammed. An engine rumbled to life. A few moments later, a police siren blasted. Jack could envision what happened. One perp had made his getaway, and the officers were giving chase. Hopefully, they wouldn't be too late. It had taken too long to get back to their vehicle.

He and Nicole were on their own.

The woman they'd heard earlier had stopped screaming, but she was still whimpering, the high-pitched
noises of someone in pain. Or terrified. Probably both.

Nicole whipped into an open door ahead of him.
"Don't do it! Put down your weapon!"

Jack's pulse kicked up a notch and he dashed into
the room behind her and found himself staring into the
frightened brown eyes of a young Amish woman. Her
lips were cracked and dry, possibly dehydrated, and
her face appeared bloodless. Otherwise, she appeared
unharmed.

A man stood behind her, his muscular arm across
her throat. When he brushed her arm, she whimpered
again and jerked the arm away. She might have an injury
that wasn't visible at the moment. Not a break. She'd
moved the limb too quickly for it to be broken. Possibly deep muscle bruising, or a strain. Jack focused on
the young man holding her tight with one arm. With his
other hand, her captor held a knife to her neck.

"I won't go to jail," the man growled. "I'm just in it
for the money."

"Easy, kid." Jack stepped closer, then stopped moving as the knife pushed deeper into Lucy's neck. A
small drop of blood swelled against the tip. "You don't
want to hurt her. Don't make this harder on yourself."

While he'd held the young man's attention, Nicole
had managed to creep closer. Sweat broke out on the
back of Jack's neck. He needed to keep the man's focus
away from her. "Look, why don't you let her go? You
don't want to hurt her, man."

The perp noticed Nicole when she was a foot from
him. He twisted away from Lucy. That was the move
Jack had been waiting for. Lunging forward, he grabbed

Lucy and shoved her behind him, protecting her with his own body. Nicole kicked the knife away from the perp. He might have been strong, but he wasn't prepared for her move.

Panicked, the perp dove out the open window, taking the screen with him. It crashed to the ground. Jack dashed after him and climbed out, stomping on the ruined screen window, intent on pursuit.

The criminal might not have been skilled in hand-to-hand combat, but running was another matter. He hurtled over a fallen tree like a pro. Though Jack was fast, he was no match for the perp's speed. Within five minutes, he had lost him.

Turning back, he made his way into the abandoned day care, jogging, fully aware of the passage of time.

"I've called another ambulance." Nicole met him in the hallway. "I'm guessing he got away."

Jack rubbed his neck. "Yeah. The kid was fast, Nicole. And the way he hurtled over obstacles, I'm pretty confident he must have been some kind of track athlete in high school."

She tilted her head, considering.

"Could be. We got a good look at him. He didn't seem old, only sixteen or seventeen, I'd guess, so we can definitely look into that and check with the local school districts. Officer Hansen called. They're on their way back. By the time they'd reached their cruiser, the perp had too much of a lead. I'm going to have them wait here for the investigation team."

He nodded. Ohio had its own unit to process crime scenes. Then he peered closer into her pretty face.

Something else was wrong. He leaned closer. "What is it?"

She glanced over her shoulder. Lucy Hilty was sitting at a kitchen table, tears seeping down her cheeks, her expression lost. In her arms, she cradled a small cloth doll dressed like an Amish girl. Like a typical Plain doll, the toy had no face. He knew it belonged to Leah. He swallowed past the sudden lump in his throat. If his young niece had lost her favorite stuffed dog, which she carried with her everywhere, she'd be devastated.

"The guy who drove off had her toddler with him. Leah is eighteen months old."

His gut clenched. They'd gotten the woman but had lost the child. And being Amish, she would have no pictures of Leah to send out. "We'll need to get an updated Amber Alert out as soon as we can get a description of the perp and the vehicle he's driving."

"I called the chief about that." Nicole looked at him. "Why are you here, Jack? The FBI doesn't usually get involved with missing person cases."

He hesitated, then motioned for her to follow him into the hall. What he had to tell her was ugly and would devastate the expectant mother, who had already dealt with more than anyone should ever have to handle. Nicole went with him, but halted a few feet from him, her arms crossed. She hadn't forgiven him. Somehow, even after three years, her lack of faith in him still bothered him.

He knew it had something to do with her childhood. Nicole never talked about her father, except in terms of how he'd hurt her mother. Knowing he was in the same company as a man she apparently despised cut him deeply.

He pushed that aside and answered her question,

speaking softly. As much as he could. His deep voice tended to carry.

"You're right, we don't usually get involved in cases like yours. However, we believe this may be linked to a group of black marketers who are involved in selling illegal arms. They are also responsible for stealing babies and children and selling them abroad."

Nicole gasped. "That's why they took Leah!"

He nodded. "Afraid so. We need to find her before she leaves the country. Once she leaves the country, it'll be virtually impossible to trace her. It's going to be hard enough because we have no pictures to send to other departments."

"That's what they said." A soft voice behind them came from the room they'd exited.

Jack and Nicole spun around. Lucy swayed in the doorway. Nicole hurried over and hooked a supportive arm around her back, then gently led her to a chair. She looked ready to drop at any moment.

Out of the corner of his eye, Jack saw the second ambulance pull in. He walked the few feet to the door and waved at the paramedics, letting them know it was safe to enter. He returned to Lucy and Nicole.

"You mean the kidnappers?" Nicole asked.

"*Jah.* The two men who took Leah and me." Her voice choked. "They said Amish don't take pictures, or go to the police, so they could grab us without worry. They also said—"

She broke down completely.

The door opened and the paramedics entered. At a gesture from Nicole, they went straight to Lucy.

"What else did they say, Lucy?" He moved closer,

but tried to stay far enough away to respect her personal space. "It's important."

The distraught woman lifted her gaze and looked from him to Nicole and back again. "They said their boss had upped the stakes. They were now kidnapping pregnant women from different communities. They'd sell our babies, and the mothers were of no use."

Nicole paled beside him. Jack pressed his lips together, horrified.

Pregnant women were being kidnapped and discarded so their newborns could be sold.

TWO

Jack could barely contain his fury. If they hadn't found Lucy when they had, it might have been too late for the sweet woman. It was clear to him that the evil men who had kidnapped her planned to do away with her once her baby was born. Would they have tried to force her into early labor? If she was dehydrated, she might not have lasted long enough to go into labor naturally. Glancing over at his former fiancée, he noted her colorless complexion and the way the corners of her eyes had tightened. Nicole understood what would have happened to Lucy, as well.

How would they find out where Leah had been taken? It was a heavy burden on his heart knowing that there were so many children out there who would never be found and returned to their parents. In fact, it was highly probable that these children were being shipped out of the state, maybe even out of the country, at this moment.

Some things he would never get used to. This kind of casual disregard for human life was one of them. No matter how many times he came across it, it always shocked him to the core and left him feeling unsettled.

The paramedics lifted Lucy to a stretcher.

"We'll follow you to the hospital," Nicole said. The paramedics nodded and wheeled the pregnant woman away.

He followed Nicole out of the structure and watched the paramedics load their patient in and drive off. He'd never been so happy to exit a building in his life. On the way out, he caught sight of something out of the corner of his eye. As he bent down, his heart slammed against his rib cage.

It was a small *kapp*, the kind an Amish child would wear. "Nicole!" he called out, and she blanched when she saw it. He heard her gulp.

"Don't touch it. Evidence." He snapped a photo and stood up again. It was hard, leaving that small head covering lying on the ground, but he knew it was important that the scene be kept as they found it, now that the perps were gone.

The officers he'd driven to the scene with, Hansen and Zilhaver, were waiting at their cruiser for orders. Nicole marched over to them while dialing a number on her cell phone. When Jack caught up with her, she held up a finger and put the phone to her ear.

"Chief?" They reached the officers. "I need to go to the hospital and check on Kathy and make sure Lucy is all right. We have a crime scene here, but it might be worse than expected." She succinctly relayed what Lucy had overheard. "I think the Crime Scene Unit needs to be prepared to search for bodies on the premises, but I have no idea how many we're talking about."

Jack clenched his jaw. So much ugliness.

He watched as she disconnected and met Hansen's shocked eyes. The poor kid had rookie written all over him. "Look, you two wait here and meet the CSU. I need to get to the hospital. As soon as they arrive, you can return to the station and do your reports. Let me know when you leave."

"Don't you worry, Sergeant." Officer Zilhaver hooked his thumbs in his belt loops. "We'll take care of it."

"Thanks. You two are the best." She flashed them a smile. It disappeared when she faced Jack again. He winced.

She pivoted on her heel and walked away. She clearly was letting him wait with the other officers.

Not going to happen.

"Nicole! Wait up! I'd like to go to the hospital with you."

She paused, shoulders tensing, and shoved her hands into her pockets. He ignored her reluctance. He was here to do a job.

"Fine." She marched to the cruiser and got in. The engine rumbled to life. He had the feeling if he didn't hurry, he'd be standing out here alone. Jogging to the other side of the cruiser, he opened the door and brushed a few glass shards off the seat and the top of the door, then let himself in and buckled up. He'd barely settled in his seat when she backed up and expertly turned the vehicle and began driving to the hospital. The leather seat was hot against his back.

Chatter erupted from the radio. Without the window to buffer against the outside noise, Jack couldn't discriminate the words.

"Okay if I turn this up?" He reached toward the radio knob and let his hand hover until she shrugged in response. Great. She wasn't even talking to him. He listened to the radio for a moment. When nothing critical popped out at him, he allowed his thoughts to wander.

He searched his mind for something to say, but nothing came to him. Instead, the silence bloomed around them, thick with tension. He no longer sensed any hostility emanating from his ex-fiancée, only a deep sadness and guardedness.

She didn't trust him. He already knew that. No matter how many times he'd tried to think of what he could have done differently, he always came up blank. He was doing his job. The same way she did hers, day in, day out. Yes, sometimes his work required some deception, and he was not comfortable keeping things from his family. But he'd never had any illusions about what would be asked of him.

Only about what it would cost him.

He winced, then grabbed his phone to distract himself from the coldness coming from the woman he'd once thought he'd spend the rest of his life with. He started to send a text to the woman watching his niece, when his phone rang. He instantly recognized his babysitter's number.

"Hello? Joyce?"

Nicole stiffened beside him.

"Uncle Jack, when are you coming home?" Chloe's sweet voice responded instead of Joyce. He blinked. Why was she calling him?

"Hey, kiddo. I'm at work. Where's Joyce?" He was aware of Nicole listening in. She had no idea how much his world had flipped since they'd been a couple. He glanced at the clock on the dashboard. Kindergarten had started two hours ago. "Come to think of it, why aren't you in school? It's after ten in the morning."

She sniffled in his ear. His heart melted. The poor kid was only five. She'd had some hefty changes in her life, too. "Didn't feel good. Miss Joyce said I could have a sick day."

"A sick day, huh? Let me talk to her."

"'Kay. Miss you, Uncle Jack."

"I miss you, too, kiddo." He waited and heard Joyce's hello when she got hold of the phone. "Joyce, is she really sick? Do you need to take her to the doctor?"

"She had a bit of a fever this morning, Jack. She'll be fine. I think she's just missing you. This is the first time you've been gone overnight since—"

He sighed. "Yeah, since Beverly died."

Nicole gasped beside him. She knew who Beverly was, even though she'd never met his sister. Beverly and he had not had a good relationship for years. Just one more he'd messed up in his life. Maybe he was meant to be alone. Except now he had a huge commitment to his niece. Raising her, in his mind, was the only way to make up for being a horrible brother to Beverly. He prayed he'd meet her in Heaven one day to hear her say she forgave him for letting her down.

Because if it hadn't been for him, she might not have died that dreadful day three years earlier and her daughter would not be growing up without her mama.

Joyce told Chloe to go lie down and promised to read to her in a few minutes. Guilt spiraled through him. Once again, he wasn't there. But how could he rest when so much evil stalked the innocent and helpless? Sometimes, it was overwhelming.

Only God's grace got him through.

Although, lately, God had been silent.

"Look, Joyce, I'll call this evening and talk with her. And tell her I'll be back as soon as I finish here."

He hung up a few seconds later as Nicole was turning into the hospital parking lot. It was perfect timing. He wasn't in the mood to answer questions right now. Burying himself in the current case was the best way to get focused and ease the misery swimming around inside him.

Nicole parked the vehicle.

"Let's do this." Jack unfastened his buckle and let it slide back into place. He got out and waited for Nicole near the front of the cruiser. She had that look on her face, the one that said she had questions and meant to ask them.

"Jack—"

"Let's check on your partner first, then we'll go see Lucy."

She opened her mouth, hesitated, then closed it and bit her lip, evidently deciding against questioning him about his phone call. He was a bit surprised he had gotten off so easy. Forcing himself to focus on his job, he looked in all directions, his gaze scouring the parking lot as they walked toward the emergency room doors. Watching her bite that lip made him remember kisses they'd shared in the past. That was one place he couldn't afford to allow his thoughts to linger. He and Nicole were done. Not only because of his job, but also because he had Chloe to consider now.

Not that Nicole would ever trust him again, since he was still obligated to keep classified what he'd been doing the night she thought he was cheating on her.

Had she ever really trusted him? Surely, his word should have been enough.

The emergency doors whooshed open, the sudden blast of cold air blowing the cobwebs from his mind. He didn't have time to get caught up in this emotional stuff. Too much was at stake. If he didn't get his head on straight, people could die, and a child could be lost forever.

The damage to his own heart was at the bottom of his list of potential bad things that could happen.

Nicole walked around him and marched up to the reception desk, where she asked about the status of Sergeant Kathleen Bartlett. She showed her badge to the receptionist.

"She's still in surgery, Officer."

He hid a smile, knowing Nicole probably wanted to correct the woman regarding her rank. She didn't, but he knew she wanted to. He didn't blame her. She'd worked hard for her rank. She'd overlook it, because there were more important issues at hand. However, for a ranked officer to be referred to as "Officer" sometimes felt like a slap in the face.

Nicole nodded. "We need to see another person brought in here, an Amish woman. She's pregnant. Lucy Hilty."

The receptionist pointed to the chairs in the waiting room. "I was told someone would be in to talk with her. She's still being checked out. Go have a seat and I'll let you know when the doctor says you can go in."

"At least we won't have trouble finding a place to sit," Nicole muttered.

She had a point. They were the only ones in the emergency room waiting area at the moment.

"Give it time, honey." The receptionist stood with

a stack of files in her hand. "It's not even eleven. I'm going to see if I can get you an update."

She left the desk and a security guard moved into her place.

Jack and Nicole went to the waiting area. He paused while she lowered herself into a chair before choosing his. For a second, he contemplated sitting away from her but dismissed the idea. They were both adults, and such an action would look as if he were ashamed or afraid of her. He was neither.

They sat in silence for several long minutes. He thrummed his fingers against the side of his chair. The urge to move became an itch he couldn't ignore. "Listen, we might be a while. I'm going to go find some coffee."

She raised an eyebrow but didn't argue. He stood and strode off, following the signs to the cafeteria, a smaller space than he'd recalled, but he shrugged and ordered two cups of coffee. When the woman handed it to him, it was hot, just the way he liked it. He grabbed a couple of napkins, then checked out the cream and sugar options. They didn't have much. Nicole would have to be satisfied with the sugar-substitute packages and individual creamers. He crammed a few in his pocket and returned to the waiting room. Entering, he found Nicole standing at the window in a pool of light from the late-morning sun, staring out. Her gaze was so troubled and intense, he doubted she was admiring any of the gorgeous May landscaping.

"Nicole?"

She jumped slightly, then swerved to catch his eye, a sheepish grin on her face. "You startled me. I don't mean to be so skittish."

He nodded and handed her the cup of coffee and

the condiments he'd taken. "It's very hot. And all they had was plain and decaf. And they didn't have stevia."

She waved the apology away. "These are fine. Besides, I hardly expected them to have flavored coffee here. I need the caffeine more than the taste right now."

She took a small sip and made a face. He smothered a chuckle. She might not have needed flavored coffee, but he knew she was missing it.

"I called my chief while you were fetching our coffee and told him what was going on. He has requested a meeting once we're through to coordinate. I know that you're FBI and don't have to do this—"

"My supervisor, the special agent in charge, wants us to work together. We'll coordinate. And no, we don't plan on taking over your investigation. It will be a joint effort because we all want the same thing. I'll probably ask my squad mate to join us here. If these guys are branching out, he could be useful."

She smiled.

"What?"

"I forgot how wordy you get when you're irked."

"I'm not irked. I just don't want there to be any misunderstandings." He heard the defensiveness in his tone. When she smirked, he suspected she'd heard it, too.

Both of them turned when a nurse entered the waiting area and approached. "The doctor said you may speak with Mrs. Hilty, but only for a few minutes. She's exhausted and dehydrated and needs to recoup her strength before she returns home."

They agreed and followed her to the second floor. She opened a door halfway down the hall and gestured for them to enter. Nicole peered in and frowned. Jack followed after her, his eyes narrowing as they took in the second bed, closest to the door, currently empty. If Lucy stayed overnight, she'd need to be guarded. That would be easier if she were in a single room. He made a mental note to speak with the doctor in charge about it. She was a witness to an international black market racket. Which made her a target.

Just as Jack was thinking of him, the doctor came into the room. He walked past them and stopped at Lucy's bed, the one near the window. Her arm wasn't in a sling, which meant it wasn't broken or sprained. At first, she appeared to be sleeping, but when the doctor whispered that she had guests, she opened her fear-filled eyes as they halted beside her.

"Remember," the doctor told them, "don't upset her."

Jack nodded, but really, she was already upset.

"Leah?" she quavered, her eyes darting between them like a Ping-Pong ball in play.

Nicole moved closer, her hand brushing the side of the bed. "We'll do our best to find her, Lucy."

The woman didn't appear to be comforted. Why should she be? After all, she had received no assurances her child would be returned to her. That wasn't something anyone could promise her.

Lucy struggled to sit. Nicole put a gentle hand on her shoulder.

"You have to help search, Nicole. No one else knows what she looks like."

Nicole reached out and took her cold hand. It seemed so frail and shook in her grasp. Her eyes met Jack's. The tiny furrow carved into his brow was the only sign he was disturbed. She understood. Lucy would have no pictures of Leah.

"Lucy, if I get a person in here to draw Leah's picture, would you be willing to describe her?"

The Amish woman's panic-glazed eyes widened. A gleam of wild hope shone on her face. "I don't know if I can. I'd have to ask the bishop."

Jack stepped forward. "If we were to get permission from Bishop Hershberger, would you be okay with it?"

Nicole had forgotten the name of the bishop in Lucy's district, even though she'd met him in the past. Bishop Melvin Hershberger had always struck her as a reasonable man, one who considered all the options. He might not agree to their request, but he would hear them out.

"If the bishop allows it, then *jah*. I will do whatever I can to get my Leah back."

The doctor cleared his throat and fixed them with a warning glare.

"Officers, she's tired and needs rest." He moved to the door. "You have fifteen minutes. Please don't excite her."

Nicole waited until he'd closed the door and Jack had stationed himself in front of it to ensure their privacy. "Lucy, I know this is hard, but I need you to tell us what happened. Start with where you were taken."

Lucy's mouth quivered with emotion. Her voice, though, came out strong. "My husband was killed in an accident at his job two months ago. The district was helping us, but I wanted to do my part. Keeping busy helped me get through the day."

Nicole nodded. She'd never been a widow, but she recalled needing to keep her mind busy after her father died of a heart attack and they discovered all his deceptions, and then again when her mother was killed in a car accident. And after she broke up with Jack. She shoved it aside and tunneled all her focus on the small woman on the hospital bed.

"Go on."

"I started selling handmade clothes and baby blankets at a local craft store. I'd bring in a new batch every other Monday. I'd seen the man who kidnapped me there twice before. He was looking for gifts for his pregnant wife, he said. He wore a wedding ring, like the *Englisch* do. The first time he approached me, I made an excuse and left. The second time, I decided to be kind. I don't know how, but he got me talking about my husband's accident."

He knew she was a widow. She exchanged a glance with Jack. The kidnapper knew that Lucy was alone and pregnant. A perfect victim.

Lucy continued, "When I went in this past Monday, I didn't see him, but I wasn't looking for him. I wanted to hand over what I'd made and leave. I got back to the car where my driver was and—"

"I know. You can skip that part." Nicole already knew that the young driver had been murdered, his throat slashed.

Lucy said, "I didn't see their car until they jumped out and grabbed at me. They jabbed me with a needle. I felt dizzy, then I fainted."

She'd been drugged. Nicole fought to keep her face smooth, even as her pulse thundered in her ears.

Lucy continued her gruesome story.

"When I woke up, I was in the place you found me and my head hurt. I tried to get away this morning. The one called Ted had left the door unlocked. I grabbed Leah and made it outside. They came after us and Ted took Leah from my arms. I yelled at him."

She sobbed and a tear dripped from the side of her face to the bedsheet. "That's when the other man twisted my arm. He had a gun and forced me back into the building. They wouldn't let me see Leah again. Ted told me they would hurt her if I tried to escape."

That must have been when the caller had spotted her. She'd seen him hurt her arm, and then Lucy had been taken back inside the house. At least they knew Leah was still alive and unharmed as of eight o'clock this morning.

"What happened next, Lucy?" Jack's quiet voice broke in gently.

"When the police arrived today, the man I'd talked to at the craft store grabbed Leah and left." Lucy closed her eyes. "He told the boy to forget about my baby and kill me so I wouldn't talk to the police and meet him at the rendezvous point."

Nicole caught her wording. "Lucy? You said, 'He told the boy'? Were they both teenagers?"

Lucy shook her head. "*Nee.* The one who ordered Ted to kill me was an adult. Maybe your age, or so."

Hearing Lucy talk about her near death so calmly sent a chill sweeping up Nicole's spine. She nodded to Jack. He stepped in and began asking questions about the men who'd taken her. Nicole sent a quick text to her chief, requesting a guard on Lucy's door. When the doctor entered a few minutes later, Jack was wrapping up.

The doctor returned, his glance taking in the distraught woman on the bed. Without a word to them, he moved to her IV and injected something into the line, telling Lucy it was safe for her baby. Within a minute, Lucy's lids began to droop, even while she struggled to remain awake.

"We'll leave you now," Nicole whispered to Lucy. "Sleep well, my friend. I'll be in touch."

Lucy's eyes closed completely. Her breathing grew deep and even. She was asleep.

Jack followed the doctor out of the room. When he came back in, Nicole was standing near Lucy, watching her sleep. Jack motioned for her to join him in the hall.

Nicole closed the door behind them as they exited the room.

"I asked the doc if he could move her to a private room. He said he'd make sure no one else was placed in this room so if she needed it, someone from her community could stay with her in the other bed."

Relieved, Nicole smiled at him. He blinked. "Thanks, Jack. I was thinking the same thing—that she shouldn't have another patient placed in there with her."

"I'm wondering if it would behoove us to request someone stationed at her door?" Jack murmured.

"I already took care of that." Nicole held up her cell phone. "My chief is sending someone over immediately. He wants us to hang out here until they arrive."

They stood in the hallway, awkward, until they heard the steady sound of hard-soled shoes slapping the tile floor. An officer came around the corner and greeted them.

"I guess this is my station," the young man quipped, grinning.

"There is a very fragile young woman in this room who's in a lot of danger." Jack speared the young man with his gaze. Nicole thought he was deliberately trying to be intimidating in order to emphasize how serious the situation was. She couldn't blame him. This officer the chief had sent had green written all over him. He was a good man and had promise. Still, it wasn't the choice she would have made.

"I know that, sir."

"I don't need to tell you to stay sharp," Jack pressed, his stare fierce.

"No, sir. I know my job."

Nicole caught the edge of resentment in the young officer's voice. "You got a problem with what Special Agent Quinn said, Beck?"

He straightened at the snap in her tone. "No, ma'am."

"I'm glad to hear it. Make sure you remember that."

Nodding, she pivoted and headed to the door, aware with every step that Jack was at her side. She hadn't meant to lose her temper. But there was more at stake here than anyone's feelings. A child's life, and possibly a young mother's, were in danger. There was no room for mistakes.

Striding out to the car, she unlocked it, then slid behind the wheel. She waited for Jack to get in his side.

"Are we going back to the station to get a different vehicle?" Jack pointed to the missing passenger window.

She hesitated briefly, then shook her head. "I think we need to head out to the bishop's house to get his permission to send a forensic artist out to see Lucy. If we go to the station first, we'd be backtracking and lose too much time. This can't wait."

He glanced at her. "Could someone else go talk with the bishop?"

She shook her head. "He knows me. I think it will go smoother if I approach him then someone he's never met."

He tilted his head in thought then nodded. "That makes sense. I trust your judgment."

She started the engine and left the parking lot. "The bishop's house is about half an hour from here. We should be back to the station around one-ish this afternoon."

"That should give me plenty of time to call my SAC and update her. See if Tanner can join me on the ground here."

She rolled her eyes. The FBI and their initials. She knew that SAC stood for the special agent in charge. It would never have occurred to him to refer to her as "my boss."

"Fine. I'll never turn down more help. Not if it will bring a baby home." She'd never been one to fight over jurisdiction. Nor would she risk a life because she and Jack had a history. She'd work with him, keep it professional, then she'd shoo him out of her life again and wipe her hands clean of the whole thing.

She could do it.

Jack stared out the gap left by the missing window, his fingers lightly tapping the door panel while he hummed under his breath. Her hands tightened on the steering wheel. "Revelation Song." She'd heard him sing that song before. It had always touched a chord deep within.

She took a deep breath and focused on the road. The next twenty-five minutes were quiet. Finally, she pulled onto the bishop's road.

"Bishop's house is just ahead." She flicked on her blinker and turned into the drive leading to the bishop's modest white farmhouse. His wife, Edith, stood at the clothesline, hanging up a load of freshly laundered garments. The gentle breeze blew the line of dresses, aprons, shirts and trousers. It was a peaceful scene, one she hated to intrude upon, even as she parked the cruiser and stepped out into the bright late-spring day.

"Nicole." Bishop Melvin Hershberger called from the back door. "Have you news of Lucy Hilty?"

She nodded. "We found her. She's in the hospital, under guard. She is dehydrated but should be able to return home tomorrow."

Edith Hershberger joined her husband, an empty basket resting on her hip. Her blue eyes were worried. "You have not mentioned her *dochter*."

"The men who abducted them still have her," Jack replied, his tone soft.

"This is Special Agent Jack Quinn. He's helping out. The men who abducted Lucy are dangerous kidnappers who are responsible for several other abductions and will possibly be back. We need to find Leah. Bishop Hershberger, we are here to ask permission to allow a forensic artist draw a sketch of her to disseminate."

She held her breath while he pondered her request.

"*Jah.* This I will allow. We need to bring Leah home. When will Lucy return to her *haus*?"

Jack cleared his throat. "I don't want to alarm you, sir, but Lucy is in danger. Grave danger."

The bishop frowned, not angry but resolute. "She can remain with another family when she returns."

Nicole wanted to push, but his face was set. Two minutes later, she and Jack were back in the cruiser returning to Sutter Springs Police Department. They turned onto a long and winding two-lane country highway. "Why didn't you press him to allow protection for Lucy?"

She chuffed in disbelief. "Seriously? You haven't been gone that long, Jack. Allowing us to use a forensic artist is a huge concession. To let in a protective detail would mean letting in officers armed with guns. Amish don't believe in using weapons against other people. I didn't want to lose the concession he had already made."

"Huh." He rubbed his chin, then sighed. "I understand that. I'm just not happy with the idea of sending Lucy home while the abductors are still out there."

Nicole took her gaze off the road for a moment to peer at him, struck by the sorrow she heard in his voice. She remembered him saying his sister had died and wondered if there was a connection there. About to open her mouth to ask, she froze, arrested as Jack's expression twisted in horror.

"Look out!" He reached over and jerked the wheel to the right. She whipped her head around in time to see a crop-dusting plane headed in their direction, nearly on top of them.

"Why is he flying over the road!" Nicole spun the wheel, sending the cruiser off the road and skidding into the grass while the plane passed them. She knew the pilots sometimes flew as low as eight feet above the crops. She'd never seen one up this close before. She hit the gas and her tires spun in the grass and mud before finding traction again on the paved road.

Her questions were answered when the plane did a staggering loop in the air and roared back toward them. She floored it, trying to outrun this new threat. Bullets rained down on the road from the craft.

They'd become the killer's new target.

THREE

"Go, go, go!" Jack stamped his foot several times on the floorboard as if he could hit the gas and help the car move faster.

"I'm going," Nicole yelled back, jerking the wheel in a zigzag pattern to avoid the plane's third pass.

His hand gripped the handle above his door. The plane was nearly on top of them, its small engine roaring. The rear window shattered.

"If he hits a tire, we're toast," Nicole yelled above the droning.

The plane zoomed past them. The cruiser rocked. That was too close. He gripped the handle tighter. He hated having so little control of the situation. Nicole was a good driver. But there was only so much one could do when bullets rained down from above and you were out in the open.

It would be back. Of that he had no doubt.

An intersection loomed ahead. "Wait, isn't there a long bridge on that road?"

"Brilliant." She jammed her finger on the call button. When the phone was picked up, she spoke over the person's greeting. "Chief! We're being chased by shooters in a crop-dusting plane. Coming up to the Smart Shore Covered Bridge."

"I'll get backup there, Sergeant. Just get to the bridge and we'll take it from there."

He clenched his jaw as she took the turn at full speed. The cruiser actually tilted as the wheels on the left side of the vehicle lifted off the road. Seconds later, they re-settled, and the car shuddered with the impact, slight though it was.

Jack pulled his weapon out of his holster.

"What are you doing?"

He glanced at her. "Nothing foolish, I promise. But if they force us to stop, I want to be ready to defend us."

"If we can hold on for a couple more minutes, we'll be good." She ducked her head a bit, angling it to see beneath the visor. "If we can make the bridge before they come back—"

The low hum of the airplane zooming toward them canceled that wild hope. The plane was looming low in the sky. If it passed them, it might clip the lights on the top of the cruiser. It would be close.

A horn blared, the unmistakable loud and long trum-petlike blast of an 18-wheeler. The small plane's nose rose. The aircraft lifted and sailed away from them. Nicole edged over to hug the side of the road as a huge silver-and-red semitruck barreled past them, stirring up a cloud of dust in its wake.

"There's the bridge!" Nicole pulled one hand off the wheel to point, her fingers shaking. She immediately slapped it back on the wheel.

Jack shifted in his seat to glance back over his shoul-der. He winced at the second broken window. Glass peppered the entire back seat, the small shards glittering like diamonds on the black carpet of the floorboard.

A few seconds and that might have been the front windshield. He and Nicole would never have survived it. Not for the first time, he wished he could cushion her from all harm.

Then his thoughts turned to his niece. What would she do if something happened to him? She'd had more than enough turmoil in her young life. The desire to hear Chloe's voice surged inside him. Later. He'd call to check on her the first moment he had time.

The plane dropped again, coming at them from behind. He tore his mind away from his niece and Nicole and gave all his attention to their current predicament.

"Here he comes!" he yelled. In horror, he saw a couple of cars ahead of them. If they didn't move, either Nicole would hit them, or they might be struck by flying bullets.

Please, Lord. We need Your help.

Nicole switched on the lights and the sirens. The wail filled the air. Within seconds, the drivers had pulled to the side. He released the breath he'd been holding. The cruiser raced down the street toward the Smart Shore bridge, a large wooden structure that was only wide enough to accommodate one normal-sized vehicle. Large trucks were routed around the bridge, as it was built long before they began coming through Sutter Springs with any regularity.

No way was a plane, not even a tiny one like a crop duster, fitting inside the structure. Hopefully, no one was in the bridge coming from the opposite direction. They zipped past the signs warning of a single lane ahead.

Their lights flashed into the dim interior of the bridge. It was empty. Jack sent a prayer of thanksgiving up as Nicole gave it all she could.

They shot under the cover of the bridge. Just in time. A shower of bullets pelted the roof of the structure, sounding like little explosions.

"We should wait here until the backup sent by your chief comes," Jack said.

Nicole threw him a glance. "Ya think?"

He nearly smiled, the sarcasm relieving some of the tension building as adrenaline flooded his body.

Her eyes refocused on the end of the bridge. "Speaking of the backup…"

He saw the flashing lights at the other end even before he turned his head. "They have impeccable timing."

It was a relief to leave the bridge and follow the cruisers to the Sutter Springs Police Department. The two law enforcement vehicles must have been enough to scare off their pursuer. The crop duster was just a distant roar by the time they made it into the open.

"The plane targeted us," he said, noting the obvious.

"I know. It gave up when the other cars arrived."

"That was an awfully risky move—why go after us like that? Why not focus on getting away?"

"It feels…personal," she said, and he had to agree. Whoever had shot at them seemed motivated by rage and was not thinking things through. There were easier ways to mess up the case than trying to take out law enforcement. There was a lot of jeopardy attached to that kind of action.

He tamped down the unease crawling up his spine as they drove to the police department. They could be dealing with someone erratic.

Part of him felt like he was coming home as they neared the station. He'd spent several years working there, building friendships, some that were still strong.

The one that really mattered, though, had been damaged beyond his ability to repair.

He wouldn't think about that. He needed all his wits about him to outsmart these villains and save a little girl. Hopefully, putting a spoke in the wheels of a human trafficking and terrorist group while they were at it.

Nicole pulled into a spot and killed the engine. When they got out of the vehicle, he put a hand on the roof to steady himself for a moment.

"Jack?"

He grimaced. "I'm okay. Just an overload of adrenaline. I think I'm going to need some sugar when I crash."

A soft laugh floated across to him, and his throat tightened. He'd missed that sound these past few years. The way she had greeted him a few hours earlier, he didn't think he'd ever hear it again.

"I think we can stop by the vending machine on our way to meet the chief." She made good on that promise when they entered the station, heading to the break area and waiting while he made his choice.

"Do you need something? For your diabetes?"

She shook her head. "I have a snack at my desk. I'll snag it on the way."

Jack followed Nicole down the center of the station, moving between desks. Several officers called out greetings. He waved back. He passed the desk where he used to sit. It was covered with a tumble of papers and files, several empty plastic pop bottles grouped near the back. He blinked. It felt wrong. He'd kept his desk neat enough to eat off when he'd sat there.

Nicole grabbed an apple and a protein bar when they got to her desk. It was the same as she'd always kept it. His eyes lit on the small ceramic kitten sitting in the back corner. He'd gotten her that. Surprised that she'd kept it, he glanced at her. She met his eyes then looked away, flushing. Unsure what it meant, he remained silent.

"Sergeant. Special Agent. In here." Chief Spencer stood in the open doorway of the large conference room. He stepped aside to allow them to enter ahead of him, then shut the door before joining them. "There's coffee if you want it."

Jack walked to the Keurig and made himself a cup of French roast, adding two creams. "Nicole?"

She nodded. He made her one, too, adding in the sugar substitute and cream the way she'd always taken it in the past. She thanked him and took a sip, nodding when it met her approval.

Jack sat beside her without thinking.

He froze. It was a large table. He could have placed himself across from her or at a number of different chairs. It was done. He'd look foolish moving to a different chair at this point.

He wanted to look and see her reaction but didn't dare. In his periphery, though, he saw her fingers tighten on her coffee mug.

Clearing her throat, she turned her attention to the chief.

He forgot his resolve and peeked at her. Her cheeks were still pink, her gaze direct. Her dark brown hair was pulled away from her face in a long ponytail, which waved down her back.

He puffed his cheeks and blew out a breath, hard. Man. She was still one of the prettiest women he'd ever seen. She rarely blushed, though.

"Sir." Nicole addressed the chief. "Have you heard anything about Kathy's status? Or about the plane that attacked us?"

Chief Spencer settled his bulk, all muscle, into the chair at the end of the table. "I haven't heard anything about the pilot or the plane yet. I'll not keep you in the dark when I do. I'm fairly certain we'll find that it was stolen from a local farm. Too easy to trace otherwise."

They both nodded their agreement. It would make sense. The attack happened so soon after Lucy was rescued, the plane had to have been from somewhere close.

The chief took a sip of water from a plastic bottle before continuing.

"As to Kathy, they had to do surgery on her. She's going to be out of commission until the doctor okays her. And she will have to be on desk duty until she's had physical therapy and is up to regulation again. You know how that goes."

"You know I was driving her cruiser." Nicole shifted in her seat. "It took quite a beating today. Two windows shot out, some dents."

He nodded. "It'll be taken care of."

The chief switched his gaze to Jack. "Jack, it's good to see you again. I understand from your supervisor that our kidnappers and the perp you're hunting might be the same person."

"Yes, sir."

"You know we're a small police force here. And we

are down an officer. Since we all want the same thing, I am taking advantage of your presence. A child's life is at stake. I'd appreciate it if you could partner with Nicole on this case."

Nicole choked on the sip of coffee she'd just tried to swallow. Partner with Jack? Work with her ex-fiancé? She'd had no choice this morning, however, she hadn't expected them to be teamed up once they arrived back at the police department. Chief Spencer was aware of her history with Jack. Wildly, she stared at her boss, hoping he was merely trying to ease the tension.

Nope. He was serious.

She clenched her jaw tight, resisting the urge to jump up and protest. It would do no good. He wasn't asking her opinion. He was making a decision about what he believed would be the best course of action.

The most efficient way to find a lost child before she was taken out of the States.

Nicole wouldn't allow her own selfish desires to take precedence over a child's well-being, either. She schooled her features into her calm mask. She had practiced it in front of a mirror as a young officer to help her in situations like this.

"Do you have a problem with this, Sergeant?"

It wasn't really a question. She would do the job she was trained to do, and she would do it well. Then she'd send Jack back to Columbus, Ohio, where he belonged, and she'd stay here. End of story.

Except it wasn't going to work out that way. She bit back the sigh aching to escape.

"No, Chief. No problem."

"Good. Jack, I want access to whatever files or information you're allowed to share. Anything we get could help us to put these guys behind bars."

"Chief, I was also planning on asking my SAC if my squad mate could join us. Tanner's a whiz with details and data. He could be a huge help."

Would he work with his partner, then?

She was shocked at the tiny spark of disappointment that flared, then quickly ignored it.

"Sounds like a good plan. I'll not refuse the help, as long as you all remember that I'm in charge here."

"Understood."

"Good." The chief stood. "Why don't you call her now? Then, when your colleague arrives, he can help with the intel and planning here while you and Sergeant Dawson do the footwork."

Nicole sank back in her chair, a bit rattled at the tiny spark of relief swimming in her gut that she and Jack would be working together again. Surely, the only reason she would be happy about that was because she didn't want to search on her own. It wasn't efficient and there was too much to lose.

She squirmed in her seat, unable to completely convince herself of her reasoning.

Enough. It was irrelevant anyways. The chief said they would be working together and that was the end of it.

A thought struck her. "Oh, I almost forgot." Nicole leaned forward in her seat. "Before all this with the plane, we stopped in to see Bishop Hershberger. He gave us permission to have pictures drawn of Leah."

The chief rubbed his hands together, his expression fierce. "Now we're getting somewhere. You should talk with the artist, too. Did you get a good look at the two perps?"

"Yes and no. I got a look at the one, but the other I didn't have a clear view. I think I saw him when I looked at the building from the outside, but not well enough to identify him."

"Well, one is better than nothing. I'll see what her availability is." He strode from the room, leaving Nicole alone with Jack.

Jack was already on the phone with his supervisor. Tilting her head, Nicole tuned in to his conversation, allowing her eyes to rest on his face. He hadn't changed much since she last saw him. An extra line or two around his eyes and a few gray hairs sprinkled his short dark brown hair at his temples. Other than that, he looked the same.

Except that she hadn't seen him smile since he'd appeared that morning. Granted, it had been a harrowing and rather dismal day, but Jack had always been the man with a smile and a joke to smooth the way or cheer others up.

Not now.

What had happened to him to change him that much?

Then she recalled him talking about his sister, and her stomach dropped. How had Beverly died? She'd never met the woman, but she had heard much about her. Jack had always felt responsible for her poor choices, and nothing Nicole ever said had made a difference.

"Great!" Jack ran a hand through his hair, leaving a trail of disheveled strands. "I'll keep an eye out for him."

Hmm. Apparently, she missed something. Probably his squad mate would be on his way soon. She'd have to ask for that information. She hoped he wouldn't take too long to arrive.

He disconnected the call and met her eyes, raising his brows in question. She flushed. He'd caught her staring.

"So," she began, anxious to know what was next. "I assume your squad mate is on the way?"

"You got it. Tanner is actually already en route. I guess when the chief spoke with my SAC earlier, she made the call to send him out. He should be here within the next two hours or so."

She nodded. Columbus was less than three hours from Sutter Springs. She stood, her muscles tense and twitching, needing to move.

The door swung open, and Officer Hansen stuck his head in and looked at Nicole. "Hey, Sergeant Dawson. Chief Spencer asked me to tell you the forensic artist is on her way to the hospital."

Her eyes widened. "How did that happen? We always have to wait for her to become available."

He shrugged. "I don't ask why when things go my way. Just accept it."

"Smart man." She turned to Jack. "What say you we head over now and deal with the artist? The sooner we get pictures circulating, the better."

He nodded. "Sounds like a plan. Want me to drive?"

She recalled the last ride and shivered. "Actually, yes. I could use a break."

Plus, it might not hurt taking a different vehicle. They were targets, too, now that they had seen the perps. She couldn't identify the second guy, but he didn't know that. No doubt the men who'd attacked earlier would be on the lookout for a policewoman in a Sutter Springs cruiser. Kathy was the only other female street cop in the department, and she was in the hospital.

Another shiver worked its way up her spine. She could come face-to-face with him and not know it. In such a situation, she had no doubt she'd be dead before she realized her mistake.

FOUR

Francesca Brown, the forensic artist the Sutter Springs Police Department and half a dozen others contracted with, was waiting for them under the hospital carport when Jack swung his silver Ford Escape into the visitor parking lot. He'd expected her to meet them inside, where it was air-conditioned, instead of standing outside in the heat. Normally, the temperatures in May were mild in Sutter Springs, Ohio, but this year May was unusually hot. The midafternoon sun beat down relentlessly as he and Nicole left his vehicle and made their way to her.

"She hasn't changed much," he mused.

"Maybe not on the outside," Nicole whispered back. "She has had a tough year. Her husband was killed in a hit-and-run last spring."

He winced. "Thanks for telling me. I would have asked about Sean."

She nodded, but they were too close to say more.

"Fran, it's been a while." Jack stopped several feet from his former colleague. "I hope you haven't been waiting for us too long in this heat."

"Jack." She stretched out an elegant hand complete

with manicured nails to shake his. Her grip was strong and sure. "Good to see you."

There was a question in her eyes as she turned her head to Nicole. He flushed.

"It's all good," Nicole said, preempting any discussion about working with her former fiancé.

"Glad to hear it." She returned her gaze to Jack. "Hospitals make me tense. I prefer to go in and do my job, then leave."

He shoved any and all questions aside, instinctively knowing her husband's death was a large part of her stress.

"We have a young pregnant Amish woman in there," he began. "Her child has been kidnapped and there are no pictures of the little girl. Nor do we have a picture of one of the perps, the man who has her. Lucy can help us with both."

The three made their way inside the hospital, flashing their badges when they arrived at the front desk. The clerk let them proceed to Lucy's room.

"You said one of them? How many were there?"

"Two." Jack stopped outside Lucy's door. Beck was still standing guard. Jack addressed him. "Any issues, Officer?"

"No, sir. Mrs. Hilty is resting. A nurse checked on her five minutes ago."

"Excellent."

Nicole put her hand on the doorknob. "Both Jack and I saw the second man, Fran. So, we can work with you back at the station if you'd like."

Fran grimaced. "Let's see how this goes first."

Nicole pushed open the door and let Francesca enter before she followed. She froze inside the entryway. Jack nearly ran her over. He stumbled to a halt, placing his hands on her shoulders to catch himself.

Lucy Hilty lay on the narrow hospital bed, shaking uncontrollably, her lips blue. A thin line of saliva bubbled up from the edges of her lips and dribbled down her face.

Jack dashed to the bed. Behind him, Nicole rushed through the door and yelled for help. Thankfully, the nurses' station was less than fifty feet from the door to Lucy's room. Within twenty seconds, the first nurse burst inside the room, followed closely by a young doctor.

Jack and Nicole stepped aside as the medical personnel leaped into action. A nurse unhooked the IV.

"This fluid doesn't look right." She showed it to the doctor. "When I looked at it an hour ago, it was fine."

Beck gulped, a loud sound which garnered everyone's attention. "Um. Another nurse was here a few minutes ago. She fiddled with it."

"Describe 'fiddled,' Officer."

Unlike earlier, when the young officer had responded to Jack, not a hint of disrespect or arrogance colored his voice or manner. "She had a needle, sir, like when you get a shot, and injected it into the bag."

"Poisoned." The doctor immediately ignored the officers and barked orders to his team.

"Beck." Nicole stepped toward the door. "You're with me. We need to scour this hospital and find your nurse, if she's still here."

He nodded eagerly. No doubt he was intent on making up for what he perceived as a failure to do his duty and protect Lucy. Jack would feel the same way.

They hurried from the room, leaving Jack and Francesca behind to keep watch over Lucy. Jack whispered a quick prayer for the young Amish woman and her baby. His mouth went dry, as if he'd tried to swallow a wad of cotton balls. Had they alerted the medical team in time? Or would he watch his sister's fate play out again, right before his horrified gaze?

He hadn't arrived in time to save his sister. The poison she'd ingested had already worked its way through her system. The investigators declared she'd killed herself. He knew better. She'd told him she was in trouble. Her fear was the only reason she'd broken three years of silence and begged him for help.

Jack had dropped everything and driven as fast as his car would go. He'd still been too late. She'd lifted her lids when he'd called her name, her gaze unfocused, pupils dilated. She had just enough life left to speak one last time.

"Forgive me. Take care... Chloe."

And then she was gone. His baby sister, the last member of his family except for the tiny, bewildered little blonde girl with huge blue eyes filled with fear.

He shook his head and returned to the present, watching and praying as the doctor worked to save Lucy and her baby. Grabbing his phone, he called the Ohio State Police, requesting detectives from their Crime Scene Unit. Then he sent Nicole a text, letting her know someone from the CSU was on the way.

"This is horrible. What do you want me to do?"

He startled. Francesca. He'd forgotten she was even here when he sank into the past. Part of him wanted to let her go, knowing she was uncomfortable in the hospital setting. But what if Lucy revived? This might be the only opportunity they'd have to get the pictures drawn.

When or if she came to, she'd want to know they were doing all they could to find her daughter.

"Tell you what. Why don't you wait in your car, or in the cafeteria? I know how hard it is to get you here, so if she is able to talk with you today, I'd like that to happen."

She frowned, clearly unhappy. If she refused, he wouldn't try to stop her. Finally, she came to a decision and nodded. "Fine. I'll go to the cafeteria. I could use some coffee to settle my nerves. Call me if I need to come back. I won't leave until I hear from you."

"Sure." His attention was already back on Lucy. Her color was looking a little better. Hopefully, Nicole was finding success in her search for the poisoner.

There was nothing left for him to do but wait.

Nicole and Officer Beck dodged through the halls of the hospital, stopping to ask the staff if they'd seen anyone who fit the description of the nurse Beck had seen entering the room.

"I'm so sorry! I can't believe I didn't realize she wasn't a nurse."

"You said she was dressed like a nurse?" Nicole kept her voice reasonable, continuing to speed walk down the hall.

"Well, yes. She had on scrubs and a name badge."

"Then stop blaming yourself and focus on finding her. You at least have a chance of recognizing her face. I doubt she'll be in scrubs still. So, look at the faces, the eyes and try to recall the small details."

She'd just about used up all hope and optimism she had when Beck hissed beside her.

Straightening her shoulders, she glanced at him out

of the corner of her eye. Keeping her voice low, she breathed, "You see something?"

"She's still here." He spoke out of the side of his mouth. "The woman in the gift shop. She's waiting us out, I'm sure of it."

It made sense. She'd probably seen them coming and ducked inside to hide. Maybe she'd heard sirens, caught sight of flashing lights. Well, the game was up. In spite of her efforts, they'd found her. Her scrubs were gone, replaced with jeans and a dark T-shirt. She was average height, maybe an inch or so shorter than Nicole's five foot seven, and had pulled her medium brown hair back into a ponytail held together by a black hair band. Her face was devoid of makeup, and she wore no jewelry. She wouldn't stand out in a crowd, which was most likely her goal.

"Let's see what she does if she thinks we're gone," she whispered. "I don't want to risk her having a gun and opening fire inside the gift shop with civilians hanging out."

They continued past the small store and turned around the corner. Nicole waved for Beck to flatten himself against the wall, praying that the woman would be tricked into thinking it was safe and stroll out of the hospital.

They'd be waiting to catch her if she did.

Her patience paid off. Three minutes after Nicole and Officer Beck had stationed themselves around the corner, the brown-haired woman casually strolled past them, the strap of a large tote bag over her right shoulder. She held the bag close to her body under her arm. She looked nonchalant, but Nicole could see her shoulder muscles tense under the shirt.

She was nervous.

Whatever was in the bag, it wasn't what most women carried with them on a daily basis. Nicole was sure of it. The hospital doors slid open, and she exited the building. Peering out from her hiding place, Nicole watched as the woman looked to the side, then lengthened her stride and almost ran toward the parking lot.

Gesturing for the officer to follow her, Nicole slipped back into the main corridor and strode toward the door. By the time they exited the sliding doors into the hot afternoon sun, both Nicole and Officer Beck had a hand on their weapons.

"There she is!" Nicole pointed at the woman scurrying through the parking lot, whose gaze was shooting in all directions. For a brief moment, her eyes connected with Nicole's. They widened, then she took off at a run.

Nicole bolted after her. "Stop! Police!"

Officer Beck pounded beside her. Nicole motioned for him to split off. If they could somehow sandwich her between them, she'd have no place to run. She hadn't pulled out a weapon yet, so she was probably unarmed, unless she was still carrying poison with her. A new alarm went off in Nicole's brain.

If she had any toxic substances on her, would she try and dispose of them? Maybe dump them in an area where humans or animals would be harmed? Nicole lowered her head and pumped her arms, pushing herself faster. They were gaining on the woman. She zigzagged through the parking lot, hurtling over a low concrete barrier.

"Stop!" Nicole's voice came out harsh.

The woman ignored her. Nicole hadn't expected her to do otherwise.

She reached a car and jumped inside. The keys must have been in the ignition. The engine fired up. A grating sound followed. She'd shifted into Drive with her feet on the gas. The tires squealed and the small sedan shot forward. Nicole stood directly in its path. She barely had time to leap out of the way. The bumper brushed her leg and Nicole flew backward onto the heated black tar surface of the parking lot.

Ignoring the stinging in her calf, she grabbed her weapon and shot at the tires. A pop and a strong whoosh told her she'd hit the target. Officer Beck ran toward the car at an angle and shot out the front passenger tire.

The woman's panicked face was briefly visible before she drove straight into a parked car. The other car's alarm blared, wailing like someone was kneeling on the horn.

Cautious, the officers approached the vehicle. Nicole was ten feet away when she saw the woman swallow something and drop a small vial.

"Stop her!"

She rushed to the door of the sedan. It wouldn't budge. "We need to break in!"

Officer Beck was already on his radio, calling for assistance. Nicole banged on the window for her to open up. The woman looked straight at her, a grim smile on her face, even as the seizure started.

Though Beck worked with her to get in the car, nothing budged.

By the time help arrived to give her a hand jimmying the window, Nicole had little hope. The woman's gaze was frozen in a glassy stare, her mouth slack and her body still. They might be able to save the woman, but Nicole wasn't optimistic.

What kind of twisted loyalty made someone ingest poison? Or had it been fear? Not fear of the cops, but fear of the repercussions from the ones who paid her to silence Lucy.

She couldn't think about that now. She had to keep all civilians away from the scene. Some onlookers had gathered, and she shooed them back. The team focused on extracting the woman from the car. Nicole had little hope she could be revived.

Nicole prayed she could be, both for the sake of the woman in the car and for Lucy.

While the team worked on the car, the Crime Scene Unit arrived. Nicole talked with them briefly, giving her side of the events succinctly.

"Have you heard anything regarding the search at the abandoned day care?"

The investigator shook her head. "No, sorry. The last I heard, the house had been processed and they were calling for an excavator to begin searching the grounds."

From her peripheral vision, Nicole saw the woman being pulled from the car and an officer shaking his head after a pulse and breath check.

Nicole's stomach rolled. She put an arm across her middle, as if that would steady the internal motion. "When do they think the search will be done?"

"Could be several hours yet."

When the investigator released her and turned to Officer Beck, she tugged her cell phone from her pocket and dialed the chief's number.

"What do have for me, Sergeant?"

His booming voice hit her ear and she winced. "Bad

news, sir. The woman who tried to kill Lucy Hilty is dead."

Quickly, she gave him the details of the morning.

"Well, that is bad news. How's your leg? I want you to get it checked while you're there. Also, give me an update on Lucy."

"Will do. I'll be in later today to fill in a report on the perp." She saw the paramedics moving the body of the dead woman. "Got to go, Chief. I'll try and see if I can get any information."

She ended the call, then sent Jack a text, letting him know the CSU was on the premises.

It took him just a second to call back.

"What's going on?"

She grimaced and quickly explained. He was silent for a few seconds.

"Are you okay?"

She nodded. Then felt silly. "Yes, I'm fine. The car barely touched me."

"I'm glad to hear that, but I meant emotionally, too. You've had a hard day."

His concern worked its way into a tiny crack in the armor she'd built around herself. "I'm fine. You're right, it's been a rough day. But I'll be fine."

"If you insist. Let's talk more when you come back up. The doctor believes that Lucy will heal. She won't be leaving the hospital today, though."

A second later, the phone disconnected. She almost smiled. Jack was abrupt at times, but his concern still warmed her. She couldn't forget their past history.

One of the detectives got off her phone and made her way to Nicole. "Sergeant, I thought you should know that there was no identification on the body. The car was unregistered. In fact, it had been sent to an auction house two weeks ago."

"The previous owner?"

"Deceased with no known kin."

Their one and only lead was a dead end.

FIVE

Nicole strode back to Lucy's room as fast as her bruised leg would allow, praying that the Amish woman would recover. The events of the day were starting to take a toll on her. Exhaustion weighed heavy on her shoulders, causing her feet to drag. Plus, her leg was aching, making her gait a little unsteady.

She got into the elevator and punched the button for the second floor. The metal doors swished closed, and the small box shook and jolted as it began to move. Nicole held on to the bar running around the perimeter of the car, her stomach dropping like she was riding a roller coaster at an amusement park.

Not a pleasant feeling.

When the elevator jolted to a stop and the doors opened, she couldn't get out of it quick enough. If it hadn't been for her aching leg, she would much rather have taken the stairs. She didn't like the lack of control one had in an elevator, at the mercy of whatever happened. Whether it was an electrical short or the power going out because of the storm, or just an elevator getting stuck between floors. She'd had that experience before, thank you very much, and tried to avoid being in that situation ever again.

Several nurses were buzzing around their station as she went past. None of them looked her way, but that was just as well. She didn't have time to stop. She was on a mission.

Nicole paused at Lucy's door, knocked briefly, then let herself in.

"It's me." She announced herself as she stepped completely into the room. It was empty. Panicked, Nicole ran back to the nurses' station.

"Lucy Hilty."

One of the nurses startled. "Oh! I'm sorry. I didn't even notice you passing by the desk. She's in recovery. The doctors did an emergency C-section because they were concerned about the effects of the poison on her system and her baby."

"Is Special Agent Quinn with her?"

Why hadn't Jack sent her a text or called her to let her know what was going on?

The nurse confirmed that Jack had gone with them and had told them to let her know where they were. She nodded and walked as fast as she could without running to Lucy's new location. Only when she arrived and saw Jack sitting near Lucy's bed, a look of deep concentration on his face, did she feel the knot in her shoulders begin to loosen. Then she gazed more closely at his face.

Jack Quinn looked like he'd been put through the wringer. His hair was standing on end, and deep lines stood out in relief against the grayish cast to his face. When he saw her, he shook himself out of his thoughts and smiled at her.

It pained her to see him put on a show of strength

for her benefit. She knew he was hurting, although she didn't know why.

The urge to soothe him, a man who'd betrayed their love, should have shocked her. It didn't, though. She'd loved Jack with her whole heart. That kind of connection didn't evaporate even after betrayal.

Jack put his hands on the arms of his chair and pushed himself to a standing position. He'd shed his sports coat at some point since she'd left the hospital and had removed his tie. She saw them folded up on the edge of the bedside cabinet. He glanced at his watch briefly before raising his arms above his head and stretching.

Nicole blinked. She forgotten how muscular his arms and shoulders were. Then she shook her head, disgusted with herself. It didn't matter how handsome the man was. What mattered were his actions. And in her mind, some of Jack's actions were questionable.

But she had never doubted his ability as a law enforcement officer.

"How is she?" She pointed to Lucy. The Amish woman was hooked up to an IV again, a nasal cannula providing supplemental oxygen.

Jack shrugged his shoulders. "The doctors are 'cautiously optimistic.'" He made air quotes with his fingers.

She tried to contain the smile that wanted to escape.

"What?"

She shook her head. "You used to roll your eyes whenever someone made air quotes. And here you're doing it like a pro."

He grinned at her, but it faded when they both looked back at the woman on the hospital bed. His voice was softer when he spoke. "She had a little boy. The hospital had someone call one of the Amish businesses that had a phone and they rushed out to the bishop to get permission to do a C-section. They had to have someone's permission, and Lucy's husband was dead, so he couldn't give it."

"And her son?" A fist closed around her heart at the idea that Lucy's child might have been harmed after all this.

"He's in the NICU. On a ventilator because his lungs weren't working as they should. But the pediatrician seemed to feel that was more because his little lungs weren't fully developed. His outlook is good, but the doc said had they not done the surgery, it could have been far worse."

Suddenly, she realized she'd forgotten something. Or rather, she'd forgotten someone.

"Francesca! Did she leave?"

His eyes widened. "I don't think so. I think she might be waiting for word in the cafeteria."

He looked back at the sleeping woman on the bed and frowned. "The doctor said she might sleep for a few more hours. I'd hate for her to waste her time here."

Nicole agreed. She knew the forensic artist was in high demand. Turning the issue over in her mind, she made a decision. "Let's call her in here, explain the situation and see what we can come up with."

"Agreed." Jack plucked his phone from his back pocket and tapped out a phone number. He put the phone on speaker when it began to ring.

"Francesca here."

The female voice that picked up was soft and professional.

"Jack Quinn. Listen, we have an issue here." He explained the latest development.

Francesca sighed. "I hate hospitals. Okay. I have another appointment this evening. My morning is flexible, so I will be back tomorrow. If she's not awake, then I don't have a free day until Monday."

Jack and Nicole looked at each other and nodded.

"Francesca, this is Nicole. We will do everything in our power to see that tomorrow works. We can't let this drag on."

Jack hung up. Nicole swallowed and clenched her jaw to keep from screaming or crying.

"Nicole?"

"We don't have any time, Jack. That little girl is getting farther and farther away from us, someone is out to kill Lucy, and we know that he's targeting Amish women. And that he's not alone. How can we protect them all?"

Her control broke and a tear escaped. She brushed it off her cheek and spun away from him. She struggled to regain her composure. She didn't cry at the drop of a hat.

Jack's warm hands fell on her shoulders, and he gently tugged her around and wrapped her in his arms. "I know, Nicole. I know. But sometimes there are things we can't stop. And sometimes our actions have consequences we cannot foresee."

For a moment, she burrowed into him, breathing in the clean strong scent that was uniquely Jack. It washed over her and calmed her.

But then she recalled where she was and pushed herself out of his embrace. He didn't resist. When his arms fell back to his sides, she ignored the sensation of loss that curled up inside her and backed away.

"You're right. I know you are. I hate it, though."

Anything he might have said was forgotten as an officer entered the room. "Officer Duke."

"Hey, Sergeant. The chief sent me here to relieve Beck. He said that there's another FBI guy waiting at the station for you guys, so you better get back as soon as you're able to."

"Tanner." Jack collected his jacket and tie. "Good. If he's here, we should go."

"Fine. Look, if she stirs or her eyes open, even for a second, I want to know. Understand?" Nicole said.

"Yes, ma'am."

She cast one last glance at the bed before sighing and pivoting toward the door. *We'll find her, Lucy. We'll rescue your little girl and find who's responsible for this.*

She couldn't, of course, guarantee that they'd be able to do any of those things. But she would give her all to make it happen if it was possible.

Nicole stepped out into the hall, ready to act and resolved to change the status quo on this gut-wrenching case. She heard Jack's hard-soled shoes on the tiled floor before she saw him joining her, matching her stride for stride.

"Let's go meet your friend, Jack."

The air had grown heavy while they were inside. "Feels like a storm's coming."

"Great." Nicole wrinkled her nose in disgust. He tried not to think about how adorable it was. "Let's get inside your car before the rain comes."

As the first rumble of thunder rolled through the air, they arrived at his SUV. Jack grasped the handle on the car door and listened for the click of the door lock disengaging. He never trusted these keyless locks and ignitions. It would not be a fun experience to be in a hurry only to discover that the battery on the key fob had died.

Fortunately, there was a key hidden in the fob.

Jack climbed behind the wheel of his Ford Escape, keeping a tight rein on his emotions. He didn't speak as he started the engine and backed out of his spot. He looked at the hospital carport as they drove past. His shoulder ached in memory.

"Are you thinking of when you got shot several years ago?"

His jaw dropped. He whipped his head around to see her face. "How did you know?"

She tossed him a grin, though her eyes were shadowed. "I think about it every time I see this place. It was a good thing Levi Burkholder knew how to drive."

He chuckled. He'd been with an Amish couple. When he'd been shot, the man, Levi, had shoved him into his own truck cab and driven him to the hospital, all the while being pursued by killers. Levi had left the Amish for a few years and had learned a few skills that had sure come in handy that day.

That was also the day that Nicole had rushed into his hospital room, and he'd realized that they were closer than mere colleagues.

Things had changed since then.

He tapped his turn signal and waited for a stoplight to turn green so the line of traffic blocking the exit would move out of his way. In under a minute, they were on their way, air conditioner cranked on high. He headed toward the police department, fully aware that Nicole was sitting less than a foot away, scrutinizing him with those melted-chocolate brown eyes of hers.

He refused to look in her direction, unwilling to let her see how shattered he was.

He was shaken more than he'd wanted to admit. Seeing Lucy lying there, knowing how close she'd come to losing her baby, it had all struck too close to home.

He tightened his muscles to hold back the shudder that wanted to wrack through his body, then slowly released them. A small sigh escaped, but that was it.

"What's up, Jack?" Nicole asked. "You're so tense, you'll explode if a stiff breeze hits you."

He had never been able to fool her, not since they'd met ten years ago.

He thought about lying, telling her he was tired. But he was sick of it all. The deception, the loneliness. No one knew everything about him. Not Tanner. Not Nicole. Not his SAC.

"I know you heard my conversation with Joyce earlier today. And I saw you caught the mention of my sister's death."

"Yes. I did. I never met her, but I am sorry that she died."

It hurt, talking about her, but in a way, it was also a relief, like when you lanced a blister. It was raw, but it still helped.

"She was murdered."

Nicole sucked in a shocked breath. He'd gone this far; he'd tell her the rest.

"She'd called me to come see her. I hadn't heard from her for so long. I let the call go to voice mail, not recognizing the number. I finished up what I was working on. But the moment I checked my voice mail, I took off to go to her. If only I'd listened to it an hour earlier." Even he heard the bitterness ringing in his voice. The blame and the disgust. "Well, had I gotten there sooner, we might have been able to save her. She was poisoned, like Lucy was. By the time I arrived, she was nearly dead, and my niece, Chloe, was curled up beside her, crying. Chloe was only two at the time. She's five now, in kindergarten."

Nicole reached across the console and gently grasped his right hand. He let it drop from the steering wheel to the armrest and wrapped his fingers around hers, drawing comfort from their clasped hands.

"Tell me everything." She tightened her grip. "Don't let it fester any longer."

He nodded. Of course she'd know there was more.

"They caught the man. A man by the name of Fred Johnson. He was a hired gun. He's waiting to stand trial now, which should be within the next six months. But they're still looking for the man who was behind it."

"Why did he kill your sister?"

"See, that's the question that haunts me. I hadn't had contact with Beverly in several years. I didn't even know I had a niece until my sister was murdered. And I don't know if she was murdered because of something she'd done, or if it was because of a case I'd been involved in. I can't sleep sometimes, wondering if my sister was killed as a way to make me pay."

He'd finally said the words he'd been holding inside for the past three years. Taking his hand from hers, he scrubbed it over his face. He wasn't crying, but his skin felt like it had been stretched out.

"Jack, I don't know what to say." Nicole was silent for a moment. "I appreciate your help in this and am glad you're here to assist. Seriously. But do you think you should ask for another agent to take your place here? Are you too close to it?"

Was his focus compromised, she meant.

He clenched his hands on the wheel. "Anxious to send your ex home?"

He bit the words off, immediately regretting them.

"No! I didn't mean it that way." She stiffened and half turned toward him.

He sighed, his chest heaving as a huge gust of air left him. "I know. Sorry. Look, Nicole, I need to be here. I have been following this black market ring for nearly a year. I didn't know until recently that they had gone from weapons to illegal adoptions and human trafficking. But Tanner and I have been the lead on this from the get-go. If I back out now, time will be lost. Time we can't afford. So, I will have to deal with my personal issues later."

He rolled his shoulders, letting the tension go. "Anyway, enough of that. I'm glad Tanner's arrived. Like I said before, he's got a head for technology. He's had my back since I started with the FBI."

He could have bitten his tongue at the inadvertent reference to the reason their relationship imploded, when he joined the FBI.

She didn't seem to notice. Or care. Both made him wince.

"I'm looking forward to meeting him. Another person will be helpful, that's for sure."

"He's good in a tough situation." They'd hit it off the first time they'd met. When Jack had applied to train as a special agent, Tanner had done so at the same time. They'd both been thirty-five at the time. By FBI rules, both had needed to apply and complete the training before they turned thirty-seven.

If he ever needed someone to have his back, Tanner was the man for the job.

Nicole's phone rang. She answered and put it on speaker when she saw who was calling. "Hello, Chief. We're on our way to the station now."

"Good." The chief's voice boomed. "Special Agent Hall has set up a quick presentation, and I want you both here ASAP. Between what he has managed to put together and your reports from today, we'll get everyone on the same page."

"Got it. We'll be there in less than fifteen minutes, depending how many lights Jack gets us stuck at."

He rolled his eyes.

"See you soon, Sergeant. Don't stop on the way. I've sent for pizza."

She disconnected the call.

Pizza sounded good. It had been an eventful day. Just thinking about food made his stomach grumble. Loudly.

Nicole laughed out loud. "It might be a long meeting. The chief ordered pizza so we could talk without getting distracted by hunger."

"I always said he was a wise man."

The silence that fell over them was warm and comfortable, like a blanket on a cold winter's evening. It remained until he pulled into the Sutter Springs Police Department parking lot.

"That's Tanner's car." Jack pointed at the bright red sedan in a nearby space. It stood out amid the more subdued black-and-white police vehicles. "He doesn't do subtle, as you can see."

A few minutes later, they greeted colleagues in the large conference room.

A tall man built like a bean pole with wire-framed glasses and a Diet Mountain Dew in one hand met them in the middle of the room. "Glad you decided to join the party."

Jack shook his head. "Nicole Dawson, I'd like to introduce you to Special Agent Tanner Hall. Don't pay attention to his innocent expression. He's the trouble-maker—I'm the quiet guy."

Nicole snorted and held out her hand to Tanner. Tanner switched his drink to his other hand and shook hers. His palm was icy from the can he had been holding.

"Nice to meet you."

Chief Spencer glanced their way. "Looks like everyone's here. Get your food now, folks. It's time to start."

Jack grabbed a couple of slices of pizza and a bottled water and then sat next to Nicole. It wasn't a smart move, and he knew it. He should have positioned himself away from her. The more time they spent together, the more the wounds left by her rejection would fester.

He couldn't bring himself to move, though. Sitting next to her felt natural. Besides, it would look weird if he sat away from her. They were working together.

But most of the people here knew they had a history.

Chief Mike Spencer stood and began the meeting. He switched on the view screen and all personal thoughts fled as the slide show began, displaying vivid images of lives destroyed all because of greed.

The chief put the remote control on the table. "Thanks to some great teamwork between our department and the FBI special agent—" he indicated Jack "—we have recovered Lucy Hilty, a young Amish mother who recently went missing. Mrs. Hilty is a widow. Her young daughter, Leah, is still missing. There are no photos of this child in existence. The forensic artist will attempt a composite drawing of the child and the suspects tomorrow. Until then, the only one who might be able to recognize her face is Sergeant Dawson. She's worked with this community before and knows the little girl. Therefore, Sergeant, I am making this case, and working with the FBI, your priority."

"Yes, sir." Nicole cleared her throat. "Chief, I think it likely the kidnapper has altered her appearance, so she won't completely resemble the sketches Francesca creates."

"I agree, but those sketches will be all we have to circulate." He addressed the rest of the room. "After hearing what Mrs. Hilty reported, Lieutenant Welsh and I went through our most recent missing person files. Folks, we have had three pregnant Amish or Mennonite women vanish in the past five months. That is no coincidence."

Murmurs broke out around the table.

"It sounds like they are abducting a woman every six weeks or so?" Jack tossed his theory out for consideration.

"Sounds about right." Nicole shook her head. "I'm assuming they space them out either to avoid attention or—"

"Or so they can have the child born and sell it before taking on a new one," Jack finished her statement.

The horror filling the room was tangible. Nicole wiped her palms on her slacks. How was one to combat such people?

"This has got to be stopped," Nicole coldly whispered beside him.

He agreed. No matter the personal cost, he was in until this was ended.

Before they broke for the evening, the chief had Jack and Nicole look over their records database and try to identify the kidnapper that they'd gotten a good look at. They pored over all the mug shots with no hits.

"Tomorrow, we check with the high schools," Nicole suggested.

"You're right!" He recalled the way the kid had hurtled the fallen tree. "He's probably on a track team somewhere."

"We'll check it out tomorrow morning, after we meet with the forensic artist." She grimaced.

He had no choice but to agree. The schools were closed by now. It was only one day. But that one day meant their likelihood of finding Leah had dwindled to almost nothing.

SIX

By eight o'clock Thursday morning, the temperature had already hit seventy-five degrees, and the humidity was thick in the air. Jack had stepped outside the hotel for two minutes to retrieve something from his vehicle and came back inside feeling damp. He opted for a short-sleeved polo under the sports jacket, leaving the tie behind. He was tempted to forget about the jacket, too, but brought it just in case he would need it.

He arrived at the station before Nicole and snagged a cup of coffee. It was going to be another brutal day, and he needed the caffeine to cope. She entered a few minutes after him. When he held up his cup and quirked an eyebrow at her, she shook her head.

"I already have mine."

He smiled at the iced coffee in her hand. "Let me guess. Sugar-free French vanilla. Am I right?"

"You know me well." An awkward silence followed that statement before she shrugged it aside. "My A1c has been a little out of whack," Nicole said, referring to her blood sugar levels. "I'm being very careful with my sugar and carbohydrates."

He frowned, concerned. She'd been diagnosed as

having type 2 diabetes while they were dating. They'd both been shocked. She was young to be diagnosed with the disease, although her mother had been a diabetic, as well. Although she took care of herself, he liked being there to look after her. Now that they were no longer together, no one did that.

"What do you mean out of whack? Are you all right?" He hadn't meant to fire the questions machine-gun style at her.

She rolled her eyes. "Relax. It's still controlled. I've got this. I've been on my own for a long time and I can handle myself."

"I know that." He needed to change the subject before he got himself into trouble.

Her phone rang. "It's the hospital."

He listened in as she took the call. It sounded like Lucy was awake and being moved back to a patient room. She confirmed when she'd hung up. "Her son is doing better, too, although still connected to a respirator. The hospital thinks he'll be ready to be removed in a day or so."

"That is good news. I need to text Francesca to make sure she's good to go and consult with Lucy this morning. We need to tackle that task as soon as possible."

He pulled up Francesca's number and sent her a quick message. She got back to him within three minutes, saying she was on her way to the hospital. "So, Francesca's heading out. We can meet her there."

He tilted his head and looked at her. She nodded.

"Should we take my car again?"

"I guess. I hate not using my cruiser, but if they're looking for a policewoman in a cruiser, it would be smarter, right? I mean, no one has shot at us or attacked us yet in your cute little Ford, so I say we take advantage of that."

He glared at her. "Cute! Lady, there is nothing cute about a man's car."

She snickered.

Tanner entered the room, his hair already standing on end, his familiar drink of choice in his hands.

"Tanner, I can't believe you can drink that stuff so early in the day." Jack shook his head in mock disbelief.

Tanner took a defiant swig of his Diet Mountain Dew. "Better than coffee any day of the week."

Their banter was disturbed when the chief marched in. "Are you on your way?"

"Heading out now, sir." Nicole started for the door, and Jack made to follow.

"Sergeant." They both stopped and looked at the chief.

"Have the artist do one with short hair and dressed English."

Nicole nodded, grimly. Amish women never cut their hair. She'd seen Leah once before her mother had braided her hair. Even at eighteen months, it had touched her shoulders.

The chief continued speaking. "As soon as you're done with the forensic drawing, I want you to start looking into the missing pregnant women and Leah."

"Will do, Chief." She started for the door again.

Jack followed. Surprisingly, so did Tanner.

"What's up, Tanner?"

"I talked with the SAC last night. We're going to keep our ears open. Just because our guy didn't get Lucy and her baby doesn't mean he won't go after another pregnant woman in the area."

Jack's stomach dropped. But he wasn't surprised. "I thought about that. Now that he's lost Lucy's baby, there's nothing stopping him from trying for another victim."

"Wouldn't he move on to another area?" Nicole nodded her thanks as Jack held open the door for her, then quirked an eyebrow at the two agents, waiting for them to answer.

"It's a good question," Jack said. "And the answer is we don't know. We can't rule it out, though."

Tanner adjusted his glasses. "I'm going to stick around here, keep my nose to the ground. We do have other agents, and I'll talk with Mitchell about sending them out and about to be near other communities."

"Mitchell?" She asked. "Is that your SAC?"

Both men nodded.

"Unfortunately, until a woman is grabbed, we have no way of knowing where they'll go next." Nicole sighed.

That was a problem. The Amish communities were close-knit and didn't trust the police. "I wonder if they'll report the woman missing?"

"Have all the women taken been widows?" Nicole asked as they arrived at Jack's SUV. "If they're widows or live on the outskirts of a community, it might take a few days before anyone realizes they're gone."

He didn't know. "Tanner?"

Tanner had an arrested expression on his face. "I have no idea, but it makes sense. Look, I'll see what I can find and call you with any new information. Keep your phones on you at all times."

"Yes, Dad." Jack waved him away. Tanner ran back into the station. Now that he had a specific task, he wouldn't rest until he had that final piece of information. They got in the SUV and headed out.

"It seems like an impossible job, doesn't it?" Nicole's elbow was propped on the top of the door frame, and she had her head leaned against her palm. The sunlight coming in from the window set fire to the red highlights in her dark brown hair.

"What does?" Had he missed a question?

"Finding the next victim, either before or after she's taken. In time to save her and the baby."

He swallowed. So much death and destruction. "Do you ever get tired of it, Nicole?"

"Police work?" She bit her lip, and he knew she was considering his question. "It's overwhelming at times, but I've never really thought of what else I would do."

No, she wouldn't. She'd never wanted to be anything but a cop. He remembered that.

At the hospital, they met Francesca under the carport. Jack smiled. "Feels like déjà vu."

"Hopefully with a different outcome." Francesca had her case and was already walking to the door.

Up in Lucy's room, they found her awake and anxious.

"Have you found her?" she begged them, tears in her eyes.

"Not yet, Lucy." Nicole gestured to Francesca. "Lucy, this is Francesca. She's going to talk with you and see if she can draw up a picture of Leah we can pass around, just like your bishop said we could."

It wasn't an easy process, and it took a lot of skill and patience. As Francesca and Lucy worked, Jack and Nicole walked out into the hall and stayed there on watch, not talking. They didn't want to disrupt the collaboration. They also needed to keep anyone else out.

It was almost eleven when Francesca came out of the room. She was pale and drawn, but her eyes were hard.

"I hope you nail these guys up tight," she whispered through clenched teeth.

"That's the plan," Jack replied.

Francesca looked at Nicole. "You said you saw these people?"

"One of them. The one who took the child we never saw, but Lucy did."

Francesca showed them the two images of Leah first. Nicole's eyes widened when she saw the one of Leah with her hair shortened. "That's her."

He heard hope in her voice. It was contagious, as a spark of it affected him, too.

Francesca pulled out a third sketch picture. "This one she said was called Ted."

"That's the boy who dove out the window." Nicole touched the drawing with the tip of her finger.

"We'll get a copy made of this and take it with us when we canvas the schools," Jack told them.

Francesca pulled out a fourth drawing. "This is the man who took Leah."

Jack stared at him. He was an ordinary-looking man—nothing about him rang any bells.

Beside him, Nicole gasped. "I know this man from somewhere."

Nicole stared at the black-and-white image, desperately trying to recall where she'd seen the man before. He looked around her age, give or take a year, with light brown hair and light eyes.

"Where do you know him from?" Jack asked.

She shook her head. "I don't know. I just know that I've seen him before."

She turned back to Francesca. "Did Lucy give you a name?"

"She thinks she heard him being called Nicholas."

Nicole frowned. Did she know anyone by that name? She came up with nothing and wanted to scream with frustration. So close, and then they were stopped again.

"Let's bring both when we canvas the schools," Jack suggested. "Then maybe we'll search the database again."

She groaned. "That could take hours. Why don't we pass that off to Tanner? He can do it while he's at the station anyway."

He smiled at her. "He'll hate that. The guy loves technology but searching a database can be tedious." When he scanned the picture on his phone and sent it to his squad mate, she swallowed a laugh at his mischievous expression. Apparently, Tanner's preferences weren't a deterrent.

They thanked Francesca for her time. She didn't wait around and took off. When the next officer arrived to take over the protective detail, Jack and Nicole headed out to visit the local high schools. Schools were still in session, but only for a few more weeks. The halls were teeming with teenagers counting down the days until they were freed to go on summer vacation.

The one thing about rural areas was that school districts were spread far apart. They were at least twenty to thirty minutes from one another. Nicole resigned herself to the fact that she'd likely be spending most of the afternoon in a car, zipping from school to school. Not the way she wanted to spend the day, but then, police work was seldom as glamorous as television made it.

It was almost three when they approached the fifth high school. Hopefully, they'd find someone who recognized the kid here. They wouldn't have time to hit another school today. As they pulled up, students were flowing out of the school, boarding buses and swarming into the parking lot. Between the buses and the traffic, the available parking spaces were blocked. They had to wait ten minutes for the buses to leave before they were able to find a place to park the car.

Nicole didn't like the looks some of the kids were giving Jack's car. It was a common enough make and model, but it was definitely newer and had more fancy features than most of the cars the students drove. Not to mention, she was dressed in her uniform, and Jack, even decked out in a short-sleeved shirt and black slacks, looked like the law. It was in the way he walked and the way his eyes scanned everyone and everything as if he was assessing for threats.

She sent the teens a warning glare. They looked away.

She continued toward the school. Jack walked beside her, hands in his pockets, dark glasses over his eyes. She smothered an inappropriate laugh. He looked like an FBI agent. When they reached the outer glass doors, she pressed the button to announce their presence to the office. Most schools kept their doors locked at all times to protect the students. She approved. Kids were precious and deserved to be treasured.

"May I help you?"

She leaned closer to the intercom so they'd understand her. "Sergeant Nicole Dawson, Sutter Springs Police Department."

Nicole faced the camera and held her badge up.

"Come in, please."

The door buzzed. Jack pulled it open and let her enter first before coming in behind her.

They were met in the office by a secretary, who was flustered when they showed her their badges. "I've called the assistant principal. She should be here shortly."

A minute later, a tall redhead with round glasses and bright copper lipstick entered the small office. "How can I help you, Officers?"

Nicole didn't roll her eyes, which was something of a personal victory for her. People tended to call all law enforcement members *officer*, rather than by their proper titles. It used to bug her, but she realized early on that she wouldn't be able to change it, so she let it go.

Casting a sly glance at Jack, she saw he was struggling not to smile. Yep. He was amused, too.

"I'm Sergeant Dawson and this is Special Agent Quinn with the FBI. I want to ask you if this young man looks familiar to you." She held out the composite and knew immediately they'd hit gold. The principal's eyes bulged and her mouth fell open.

"I certainly do recognize him! Jan, look at this!"

The other woman in the office scurried over, pushing her glasses up on her nose as she moved close enough to see the picture.

"Oh! That looks like Ted Adkins! Why, he dropped out last month, didn't he?"

The assistant principal nodded, horror stamped on

her face. "He sure did. Right after he turned eighteen. He only had two months to go before he graduated."

"Was he ever in any trouble?"

"No, Sergeant. He was on the track team. He lettered for three years straight. Any trouble would have been grounds to be removed from the team. He wouldn't have risked that. He was hoping for a scholarship. Then he dropped out."

Something had changed. He'd dropped out and missed his final season. The two attitudes didn't match. "Can we talk with his coach?"

Now the woman hesitated. "His coach left around the same time he quit."

That was suspicious. Nicole narrowed her eyes. "What was the coach's name?"

"Brandon Hatnells."

It wasn't familiar. "Do you have any pictures of him?"

They shook their heads. "He didn't believe in pictures. In the three years he was with us, he never had his taken. Not with the teams or individually."

Now wasn't that convenient.

They left with more questions and very few answers.

On a hunch, she showed them the drawing of the man known as Nicholas. "Is this Coach Hatnells?"

The principal frowned. "I don't know. Coach had a full beard. It's hard to tell."

They thanked the women for their time and left.

"I'm going to go out on a limb and say that I don't for a moment believe the disappearance of a coach and track star at the same time are unconnected." Jack slid in behind the wheel.

Nicole chewed on her lip. "True. I wonder how much Tanner has learned today."

"Let's head back to the station," Jack said. "We can compare notes and regroup. Hopefully, come up with a plan."

Her stomach grumbled. "And get something to eat."

He glanced at her. "Are you okay? We can stop and get something if you can't hold out."

She sent him a quick smile. Whatever his faults may have been, Jack had always looked out for her, making sure she was taking care of herself.

The fight they'd had the night they broke up came to mind. Jack had said he couldn't tell her about the woman, that it was classified. She hadn't believed him. But now she wondered if she should have. Jack had always shown himself to be a man of honor and integrity. He was scrupulous about doing what was right.

Still, did she want to be with a man who willingly hid part of his life from her for the sake of his job? Was that hypocritical? She'd never been undercover before, but she had seen undercover operations go down. They changed the officers who took them on. To be successful, the cop had to convince others that the persona assumed was the truth.

How did that not compromise your morals?

She didn't know if she could take the risk. While she believed it was possible Jack had been telling her the truth, in her heart, she feared that one day, it wouldn't always be the case.

What she really feared was the future.

She shoved the cowardly thought aside. It was unworthy of her attention, and frankly, considering the situation they found themselves in, unimportant.

"Hey." Jack's hand rested on hers. Warmth tunneled inside her. She'd missed this, his touch and the joy it brought her.

"I'm good. Don't worry about me." She carefully removed her hand from under his, aware that she yearned to wrap her arms around him and hold tight. Nicole glanced away from the hurt look flaring on his handsome face. The last thing she wanted to do was hurt him, but they had no future. And the sooner both of them faced it, the better off they'd be.

He huffed out loud beside her. Glancing at him, she stiffened. She knew that look. That was his "We're going to talk about this now" expression.

"Why wouldn't you ever let me explain what had happened?"

And there it was. She knew exactly what he was talking about. She wanted to tell him to let it go. But she knew he wouldn't. She'd have to explain. Then he'd understand.

"Look, Jack, I know you said you hadn't done anything wrong, but you were on a classified mission." He nodded, his gaze blazing into her own. She swallowed. "I grew up with a father who said one thing and did another. He led a double life. Literally. When I was fifteen, we learned that he had another family in Pennsylvania. His business trips were to visit them. After he died, his other widow came to visit us and accused mom of being his mistress. It was horrifying."

"Nicole, I would never—"

She waved his words away. "I know you wouldn't. Now. But we both have met people who are forced to live a double life to protect their cover. You have to have some acting ability to pull it off. And then there's the effect it has on them. We've seen it change them. Jack, I can't live wondering if my husband is telling me the truth or putting on an act. And it would be dreadfully unfair to you, having me wonder if you were just doing your job. You can't ask that of me."

His mouth tightened, and those blue-green eyes flashed with temper. He would never yell, though. Not Jack. Even angry, he was always a gentleman.

When he pulled into the station, she was out of the car and marching toward the building before he'd even turned the ignition off. She needed to put some distance between them. The more time she spent with Jack, the harder it was to remember that they were through.

"Hey. Wait up, Nicole." Jack jogged up to her and placed a hand on her shoulder as they went in. She could feel the heat from his hand.

"I get it. I mean, I understand your past and how undercover work can change people. It didn't change me. Look, we have to work together. Truce? We have to talk about this, though, at some point."

She shook her head. "Not now. We don't have time to waste. That's all."

Sure, it was.

Inside the station, they stopped.

"What's going on here?" Jack muttered.

Nicole glanced around, confused. All the lights were out. "We must have lost power."

Jack stuck his head out the door, then pulled it back in. "The lights are on in the building next door."

Together, they went into the main part of the station. There were four officers gathered, talking in low voices, some laughing. Sutter Springs was a small department. The chief was talking to a man at the fuse box. A few minutes later, the entire department cheered as the lights flickered and came on again.

The electrician shook the chief's hand and left. Nicole thought there was something familiar about the way he walked, but she couldn't place him. Shrugging it off, she went to the Keurig to make some coffee.

Someone had filled the water reservoir, she noted. Almost every day, she had to fill it multiple times. It was as if no one else knew how. She picked out her favorite blend and waited for it to finish brewing.

With her cup of hot coffee in hand, she sauntered back to her desk, giving Jack a glare when she saw he was sitting on her desk. He grinned and moved away. Aggravated, she plunked the coffee down, then sighed when it sloshed over the side and onto some papers she'd left lying there. She went to the sink and got some paper towels to clean up the mess.

When she returned to the room, Jack deliberately picked up her mug.

He's going to steal some of my coffee. Nicole scowled at him, then looked at the mess on her desk. It was smoldering.

"Stop!"

Jack held the ceramic mug an inch from his lips, ready to sip, when Nicole struck out and knocked it from his hand. The surrounding officers gaped at her. She couldn't speak but pointed to where it landed. There, on the new carpet the department had purchased less than a year before, the spilled coffee was smoking, burning a pungent hole through the thick carpet and charring the wooden floor.

"The coffeemaker—don't use it!" she shouted to no one in particular.

Someone had tampered with the coffee. Jack had nearly drunk it. The coffee station was open to all employees at the police department.

Whoever was after them didn't seem to care who or how many people they hurt or killed to get what they wanted.

SEVEN

Jack didn't care who was in the room. He grabbed her in his arms and held on as if his life depended on it. He could barely breathe around the fear squeezing his lungs. The coffee had been poisoned. If Nicole had drunk it, she most likely would have died. Visions of Beverly's death swam behind his eyes. He came so close to losing Nicole—again.

"Jack, I'm okay. Look at me. I'm fine."

Gradually, her voice broke through, coming as though from a tunnel. He slowly loosened his grip, allowing her to slip free. His fingers trailed down her arms and then her fingertips until she backed away, leaving him bereft.

Which was ridiculous. He tamped down on the emotions running rampant through his system. No one was watching them, except for Tanner. Everyone else was exclaiming over the corroded carpet and ruined section of the floor.

"Sergeant," the chief said, his deep voice somber. "Which coffee did you use?"

"I used the French vanilla pods, sir. But I don't think it was the coffee. The pod wasn't damaged. It had to be in the water. I also think we can't assume that I'm the target. Or the only target." She crossed her arms around her middle and looked straight at Jack. She was right. She wasn't the only one working this case. Jack longed to take her back in his arms and hold her, to comfort her and himself.

"Only one way to find out if it was the coffee."

The chief led the way to the coffee machine. The Keurig was done. The water reservoir had melted, and the clear liquid had drained out, consuming the particleboard tabletop it had been resting on.

"Acid." Jack guessed out loud.

"That's what it looks like." Her voice was mostly steady. She ran her hands down her arms as if she were freezing. "It could have been any of us. Or all of us."

"I had coffee an hour ago." Officer Beck's face had a greenish cast to it. "The coffee was fine then."

"The electrician."

All eyes turned to face Nicole. She licked her lips, still appearing shaky.

"You're right," Jack murmured. "That makes sense. No one else was here. How'd the lights go out, anyway? Smells like a setup to get inside easily."

Nicole swayed on her feet. She half staggered to a chair and sat down hard, one hand pressed against her chest. Her breathing was faster than normal and shallow. Was she going to pass out? Jack took a half step in her direction before stopping himself. As much as he wanted to comfort her, she wouldn't appreciate his calling attention to her.

He closed his eyes to get himself under control. When he opened them, he let out a breath, slowly. He walked to the table, then picked up a chair and tugged it next to her. That was all he'd allow himself. If she went down, he'd catch her and make sure she didn't get hurt. But otherwise, he wouldn't touch her.

"You okay?" he asked her, itching to take her hand. Instead, he clasped his hands together on the table.

She nodded. "Just overwhelmed. I saw him, and although I didn't recognize him, I thought there was something familiar about the way he moved. I can't say where I would have seen him. It's frustrating, but I think he's the second abductor."

"The one who took Leah." He made it a statement.

"Yes." She zeroed in on the chief. "When did the electricity go out?"

He sat at the table with them. "It went out about an hour before you arrived. I called the electric company, and they said ours was the only building affected. They sent someone right over."

He stood and strode to the phone and dialed. They heard his side of the conversation. "Yes, this is Chief Mike Spencer. I called and requested an electrician and—"

He stopped talking, his face growing grim as he listened. "I see. Someone showed up here pretending to be the electrician... Yes, that would be very helpful... Thank you... Well, if the young man does show up for his shift, I would be very interested in speaking with him."

When he hung up, his grim expression caught the attention of every officer in the room. "It seems that the electrician crews were all working on specific jobs today. There was one left to handle emergencies. He was scheduled to start later today, so they had paged him to attend us today. He never made it in. Nor did he call in and tell them he'd be late."

Not a sound issued from any of the officers. They could have all been statues as they took in this new information.

Jack broke the silence. "I hate to say it, but I think the fellow's probably dead."

Nicole made a sound as if she disagreed but didn't say anything. She was probably distressed about yet another death. Nicole was competent, but she was also compassionate and hated cruelty in all its forms. "The guy we saw, he has to be someone familiar with electricity. He was able to fix it."

"Yeah, and no doubt he was the one who sabotaged it in the first place." Tanner leaned against the windows, his face in shadows as he spoke.

"The electric company will be sending us the photo used on his work identification. We'll start searching for him, as well as for Leah and our kidnappers."

It was going to stretch their small department to the limit. In fact, if he and Tanner had not been there, it might take twice as long. The sense of rightness filled him. They were supposed to be here.

It was an added benefit that he was able to keep track of Nicole during this. Funny, her being in the line of fire bothered him so much more now than it ever had. Possibly because Sutter Springs was a fairly small and uneventful place. As far as he knew, she'd never shot anyone before.

Nor had she been on anyone's hit list.

And that was the problem. If he were to return to Columbus now, he'd be useless, always worrying about whether she was staring down the barrel of a gun at that moment or if she was hurt.

No. He'd rather be here, no matter how difficult it was to be with her and know they couldn't be together. At least when he returned home, he wouldn't have the guilt of failing someone who was important to him again. And she was very important.

A few minutes later, the PDF with the electrical worker's info arrived. The chief printed it out, read it, then passed it on to Nicole.

"Zachary Fields." Nicole read the name out loud. "Age twenty-two. He lives alone and has no relatives close by. His parents and brother live in Michigan. Okay, this is really sad. The poor kid's here by himself." She held the paper out and tried to hand it to the chief. He waved for her to hang on to it.

He heard what she didn't say. She wasn't holding out hope that young Zachary Fields from Michigan was still alive.

The chief nodded, his deep eyes hooded.

Looking around the room, Jack caught the same somber expressions on Tanner's and Beck's faces.

"Sergeant Dawson, I would like for you and Special Agent Quinn to go to Mr. Fields's home and check it out. You won't need a warrant as we have a valid reason to suspect he's suffered physical harm."

"Yes, sir."

Jack was pleased they would be together. He didn't want to be split up and worry about her the entire time. That being said, he wouldn't mind if she remained at the station. He had a bad feeling in his gut regarding the young man in question.

The destroyed coffee machine came to mind, reminding him that danger could be anywhere.

The sooner they hit the road, the quicker they could help him. If he could still be helped.

He stood and returned the chair to its original place at the table, then turned and waited for Nicole to join him. Her face still had a pinched look he didn't care for.

She would come to no more harm while on his watch. He'd do whatever he needed to do in order to keep Nicole safe and return Leah to her mother. When he went back to Columbus, his conscience would not be stained with the death of someone else he cared for.

If only he could guarantee that his heart would be whole, as well.

Hoping her legs were ready to carry her weight so she wouldn't embarrass herself when she tried to walk, Nicole stood. Jack's face had regained its natural composure, but when his gaze caught hers, she could read his distress in the tightness of his jaw.

As she clutched the paper in her hand, they left the station and got back in Jack's car. A thought crossed her mind and she smiled. She hadn't spent this much time driving around with him when they were engaged. The smile faded.

"Care to share?"

She startled. It took her a moment to understand what he was referring to. Then she realized. She'd been thinking about his car.

She glanced at him and grinned. "I was just thinking that I've spent the last two days in your car. It's getting to be something of a habit."

His eyes flashed with emotion. Her breath caught in

her throat, then he looked forward and the connection was gone. She swallowed and glanced out the window.

Jack started the vehicle and began to drive towards Fields's house. About two miles from the station, a wave of dizziness hit her.

"Nicole!" Jack's voice sounded like it was coming through a tunnel. "Are you okay? Your face is pale."

She took a deep breath and leaned her head back against the seat. "Just dizzy."

"It's probably your diabetes. Look in the glove compartment."

Nicole reached out and pressed the button. The glove compartment sprang open. Several protein bars were tucked inside. She grabbed one, recognizing her favorite brand.

"Did you put these there for me?"

He shot her a quick glance, then returned his gaze back to the road. "Yeah. It's important you eat."

Touched, she took a small bite, and swallowed hard to bypass the sudden lump in her throat. She'd forgotten that about him—the way he took care of her.

As they drove to Zachary Fields's home, she could tell something else was on his mind.

"Just spit it out."

"I know it's not possible, but I wish you could take a few days off, maybe go away, until the guy after you is caught. The airplane, the poisoned coffee…this fellow's after you."

"You're right. It's not possible. Nor is it plausible. They need me, Jack. You know how small our department is. My presence could literally be the difference between someone living or dying."

He tossed her a grim smile. "I do know that. Which

is why I'd decided to hold my thoughts to my chest, until you asked. I might not tell you everything, Nicole, but I will never lie to you."

The gibe hit her hard. She knew he was referring to her belief that he'd betrayed her or that sometime in the future he could. She wanted to believe him, but every time she weakened, she saw her mother's shattered face when she realized what a practiced liar her husband was. Nicole would not repeat her mother's fate.

Ignoring his statement, she returned to staring at the passing scenery. When they arrived at the house, she checked her service weapon before approaching.

Jack knocked on the front door. "FBI. Open up."

There was no answer. He rapped on the door again, shouting louder this time. Still no response. Their eyes met and they both nodded once. They needed to get inside the house.

Jack kicked open the door, and she aimed her weapon inside. Nothing. The walked together, room after room. In the back, a small living room, they found Zachary Fields. He'd been shot sniper-style, a single bullet to the head.

Nicole bowed her head. He hadn't deserved to die. Death was never something to be taken lightly.

On the mantel, they could see pictures coated with weeks of dust. The fridge was nearly empty, and the dishes were piled high in the sink. It looked like a college dorm room. Or the typical bachelor pad.

Jack pulled his phone up and called Tanner. "Hey, Tanner. We found Zachary Fields. DOA. Yeah. We'll need to get the names of his parents to notify them. Check on it for me, will ya? Once the coroner's done, they'll have to come and identify his body."

Nicole called in the crime scene unit investigators. And the coroner. Most likely, his family would take him back to Michigan, too. What a sad ending for such a short life.

"Third time the CSU has been called in two days. That's some kind of record," she told Jack when she'd hung up.

"Not a good record," he agreed. "We'll wait for them to get here, then head back."

When the investigators arrived, the lead marched up to Nicole. "Nicole. I have something for you."

She tensed. That was never good coming from a CSU member. "What did you find?"

"At the abandoned day care? We found a body buried in the backyard. It looked like it had been there at least three months. It was a young woman. It looked like she'd recently given birth."

"They'd been using that place for a while," Jack observed, his mouth set in a grim line.

The killers would find a new place to hole up. Considering what had occurred in the past two days, Nicole doubted they would bail on their scheme now. No, until she had Ted and his friend in custody, she'd be sneaking looks around corners.

Nicole's stomach heaved at the confirmation of their theory. She held it together, but barely, and watched the team begin their job of sweeping the place. When the coroner arrived, she told him what she knew.

"I have no doubt that he was killed by that shot." He walked around the body, taking pictures as he did. "The next of kin will need to be informed."

"We're tracking them down." Jack rubbed his hand on the back of his neck.

Nicole was ready to jump out of her skin. The second the coroner and the investigator agreed she and Jack were released, she stomped out to Jack's SUV. The vibrations of her feet hitting the ground helped her to focus on anything other than the pain and death in that house.

At the car, she paused and bowed her head, praying for Leah and Lucy and all the innocents affected by the black marketers.

In her mind, she saw the picture that had been sitting in his house. Zachary had been standing between two older people, probably his parents, and his hands were on the shoulders of a younger boy. His little brother?

The picture was several years old. His brother was nearly an adult now, but it would be hard on the family nonetheless. Their lives would be changed forever.

Jack came to stand beside her. For once, she didn't mind the warmth of his hand on her shoulder. She leaned back, drawing strength from his presence for a moment, before pulling away.

"I'm all right." She stared up into his concerned face. "Jack, I hate that we were right. I hate that there are people so greedy that they'll steal children and sell them."

He nodded. "I do, too."

"And you know what else I hate? I hate knowing that because Lucy's baby is born and she's in the hospital under guard, some other woman is in danger."

EIGHT

Jack didn't know what he could say to ease her pain and frustration. He slipped his arm across her shoulders and gave them a gentle squeeze, then dropped it before she could react. He rubbed his forearm and took a step away from her.

She shifted and cut a glance at him. "I'm okay. Don't worry. I'm not going to break down on you."

"Didn't think you would." He wouldn't have blamed her if she had. It had been an intense two days. And there were no signs of things lightening up, either.

He held open the passenger door for her, and she sank down into the seat and pulled her leg in. He shut the door and strode around to the other side and started the car. "The way I figure it, I think we've seen more action in the past forty-eight hours than Sutter Springs would normally see in five years. We're allowed to be stressed after this."

"Stress" was a mild way of putting it.

Nicole already had her phone in her hand. "You're right, of course. Let me call this in and update the chief."

Jack half listened to her side of the conversation,

but his mind was elsewhere. He hadn't been reassuring only her when he said they were allowed to be stressed.

He couldn't get his mind off the events of the past day and a half. They'd been shot at, an officer had been injured, they'd been chased by a plane manned by someone with a gun, Lucy had been poisoned, and the entire police department had come close to the same fate and now they were standing within feet of another body. All connected to the same black market operation.

It made him sick inside.

And you're worried about Nicole.

He couldn't deny it, even to himself. He was worried about her. She was in danger. But so was Lucy. And Leah? That child could be anywhere by now.

Suddenly, he needed to know Chloe was all right.

While she was on the phone with her chief, Jack disconnected his phone from the car speakers and put in a call to Joyce.

"Jack?"

"Hey, Joyce. How's my girl today?" Was it wrong that he hoped she'd stayed home from school so he could hear her voice again?

"She's fine. I drove her to school, and she didn't fuss about going in. She's resilient."

He was happy she was better but disappointed to have missed her. He'd focus on the positive, though. The last thing he wanted for Chloe was her being sad or lonely. She needed to go to school, not only to learn, but to expand her social circle. He and Joyce couldn't be the extent of it.

"Okay, tell her…" He paused. Nicole had completed her phone call with the chief. What could he say that a five-year-old would understand? And that he would be okay with his former fiancée overhearing? "Tell Chloe I love her and give her a hug for me, okay?"

"I'll do that. When are you coming home? A child needs her father, and that's you for Chloe." Oh, the guilt.

"I don't know, Joyce. I can't leave yet. There are lives in the balance here."

It sounded dramatic, but it was the absolute truth.

"Well, we'll keep praying for you and for all involved." Her voice was matter of fact. Prayer was a way of life for Joyce. He knew it wasn't a throwaway phrase. If she said she'd pray, he could trust that she'd do just that.

He disconnected the call, his melancholy worse than when he'd dialed the number.

As much as he wanted to cloak Chloe in Bubble Wrap to protect her, he couldn't. The same applied to Nicole, he realized. He would do everything to keep her safe, but at the same time, she was an officer of the law and needed to be able to perform her duties without him hovering over her.

Nicole's eyes rested on him. "You'll be able to go home to her soon, Jack. She'll be fine for a few days."

A huge lump lodged in his throat at her compassion. He cleared it. Time to change the subject and get back onto firm ground.

"Let's see what we can find on Brandon Hatnells," he said. "He's our main suspect for the second perp."

Their only subject.

Nicole's brown gaze searched his face. His ears heated. He could practically feel her glance moving over the skin on his face. He sighed in relief when she pulled her attention away from him and grabbed the laptop she'd stowed in her bag. He pulled over and let her find what she could. Then they'd know which way to head out. "I have a Brandon Hatnells." She rattled off the address.

She called in to Tanner, leaving the phone on speaker. "While you're at the station, find out where he is now."

"I'm on it." She heard clicking keys in the background. "Well, this is interesting."

"What?"

"Brandon Hatnells, at least the one who worked at the school district, doesn't exist."

Jack bumped up the volume. "How is that possible? You have to have clearances to work in a school."

More clicking keys. "He didn't actually work for the school. This is a small-town school. The track team was registered as a club, not an actual school sport. They have more relaxed rules about checking backgrounds, something that's supposed to change."

"So he slid in under the radar."

Nicole shook her head. "I can't believe that would go over with parents."

"It would if they weren't aware," Jack murmured. He made a mental note to double-check every coach or club leader Chloe would ever have.

"He was recruiting," Nicole blurted. "He was gathering people who could work for him. Who better than an athlete, someone who is physically strong?"

"He'd need to have something to hold over Ted's head." Jack thought. "Maybe some kind of debt or scandal."

"I'm going to go with the money angle," Tanner responded. "That seems to be a mighty motivator these days."

Jack winced. Had money played a part in his sister's death, as well?

* * *

Nicole watched Jack withdraw into himself. If only there was some way she could help him or reassure him. She knew he was worried about his niece. A case like this could really get to you. Especially if you were a parent or were raising a child. At times like these, being away from Chloe had to really prey on his mind. Did he feel guilty? Knowing Jack as she did, he probably did.

Casting a discreet glance his way, she was pretty sure she was correct. He looked as though he was mentally castigating himself right now. He always had taken a lot upon himself. Blaming himself for things that he had no control over.

She reached out and touched his hand. The jolt that tingled up her arm tempted her to draw back. But Nicole Dawson was no coward, so she left her hand where it was. "Hey. You hanging in there?"

He flashed her a brief grin. "Yeah, I'm good. You don't need to worry about me."

She did, though. There might not be a place for him in her life, but that didn't mean she'd successfully shut him all the way out of her heart. Deep down inside, Jack would always matter to her. She recognized that now. The way they were able to understand each other and communicate with just their eyes showed her the truth of this.

Right now, Jack was suffering.

"You know, Jack, I am glad you're here. Your being here might be the one thing that will help us find Leah before it's too late."

His brow furrowed. "How do you figure that? You're the one who knows the child."

She nodded. "True. But this whole operation is big-ger than our department would be able to handle. So, thank you."

He shrugged, his cheeks glowing. "I'm just listening to my boss. She told me I needed to be here, so here I am."

And that was the other thing to remember about Jack. He really didn't like compliments. She laughed softly. "Whatever you say."

Her voice said she didn't believe him. But she left it there. It was late by the time they returned to the station. Nicole yawned as she gathered her belongings and prepared to head home for the night. She hesitated for a moment.

"Nicole, are you sure you're okay going back to your apartment by yourself? That guy is still out there." Jack leaned his hip against the side of her desk and waited for her to answer.

His comment was so aligned with what she was thinking that she immediately denied it. "Nah, I'm good. I live in a building with security. Relax."

"I don't like it. I would prefer if I slept on your couch tonight. I don't think I could relax knowing you're alone." She raised her brows at him. "Seriously. If we find ourselves unable to sleep, we can compare notes and get a jump on the case. Be ready for tomorrow."

"Yeah, somehow, I don't see that happening."

He chuckled and pushed his chair back. She stood, too. She had her assignment and was officially off duty. Jack waved to Tanner. "We'll walk you to your car."

Nicole rolled her eyes. "You don't need to do that. It's still light out. Sutter Springs is relatively small. I'll be absolutely safe."

"Still, we're gentlemen. So, we'll walk you out."

Tanner chuckled. "Honestly, Nicole. We're heading in the same direction, so why wouldn't we?"

She laughed, her cheeks growing warm. Phrased like that, it sounded childish and petty to refuse. Jack probably knew that she was resisting spending any more time than was absolutely necessary with him. Which was ridiculous. They were working together. They had to spend time together, then he'd return to the big city, and she'd stay here.

She walked to the lot where she'd parked her off duty vehicle, a bright blue CR-V. When they approached her car, she stopped, a tingling brushing across her shoulder blades. Someone was watching her. Scanning the area, she saw no one or nothing out of the ordinary.

"What?" Jack and Tanner halted next to her.

"I feel like someone's watching us."

Neither man laughed. Instead, both removed their service weapons from their holsters and took up protective stances next to her. Jack craned his neck to peer into the back seat of her car. She was thankful she'd taken the time to clean it out two days earlier.

"We'll wait until you're in and driving before we leave." Jack continued to run his glance over the surrounding area.

She didn't lie and tell them not to worry and go ahead and leave. She appreciated the gesture.

She opened the door. "Oh! I left my backpack in the locker room. I'm sorry. I need it."

Jack rolled his eyes. "No apologies needed. We'll go in and grab it. I don't want you walking around alone, not with someone out to get you."

She didn't protest like she normally would. Being

alone when someone was hounding you was asking for trouble. Nicole wouldn't turn down an escort.

She took two steps away from her car and caught the top of the door with her hand, swinging it shut even as she continued to move toward the two agents. The door slammed an instant before the car exploded.

The blast hurtled them to the ground amid flames and debris.

NINE

"Nicole! Nicole!" Jack's voice tugged her out of the darkness. She scrunched her brows together. *Ow. That hurts.* He called her again; this time she clearly caught the panicked edge in his normally well-modulated tones.

What was going on?

Groaning, Nicole tried to sit up. Her head was pounding. Something warm and sticky was running down the side of her face. She managed to get one eye open and felt her face. It was covered with a viscous fluid. Yuck. When she pulled her hand away, it was coated with blood.

Her blood.

She was injured. For a moment, her mind was hazy, then the memory asserted itself. Her car had exploded. *Jack!* Had he been hurt? And Tanner. Tanner had been there, too.

Dragging her lids all the way open, she blinked, desperate to clear her vision. Two shapes swam and wove a foot in front of her. In an effort to make them stop, she closed one eye, a trick she'd used growing up when she'd learned she had slight astigmatism and her left eye was dominant. When the forms solidified, she saw

Tanner first, his face dirty and bloody, his shirt torn. He looked like he'd been hit by a train.

But he was alive.

She didn't even want to go near a mirror to see how she'd fared.

Next to Tanner was—

"Jack!" Without thinking, Nicole threw her arms around his neck. He rocked back for a moment before responding, sliding his arms carefully around her and squeezing.

"Nicole." His voice was rough, like he'd been shouting for hours. "I didn't think you'd ever wake up."

She snuggled closer for a second, breathing in the scent of smoke and his aftershave, relishing in the warmth of his skin against her hands, the warmth of life. Then she recalled where she was and pulled away from him. How long had she been out?

That's when she became aware of the chaos around them. Chief Spencer and Officer Beck were talking to the fire chief. She had been so dazed she had not even heard the fire truck pull up. The siren was off, though the lights were still flashing. She flinched away from the bright strobes. A couple of firefighters were spraying foam on her car.

Or what was left of her car. Her beautiful Aegean blue metallic CR-V was roasted beyond recognition. Between the thick layer of foam and the clouds of dark smoke pouring off it, it was hard to even tell what kind of car it had once been, much less what color it was.

She was alive, though. And so were Jack and Tanner. For the rest of her life, every time she thought of this moment, she'd offer a prayer of thanksgiving.

Treat Yourself with 2 Free Books!

Romance

Suspense

Get ready to relax and indulge with your FREE BOOKS and more!

Claim up to FOUR NEW BOOKS & TWO MYSTERY GIFTS – absolutely FREE!

Dear Reader,

We both know life can be difficult at times. That's why it's important to treat yourself so you can relax and recharge once in a while.

And I'd like to help you do this by sending you this amazing offer of up to FOUR brand new full length FREE BOOKS that WE pay for.

This is everything I have ready to send to you right now:

Try **Love Inspired® Romance Larger-Print** books and fall in love with inspirational romances that take you on an uplifting journey of faith, forgiveness and hope.

Try **Love Inspired® Suspense Larger-Print** books where courage and optimism unite in stories of faith and love in the face of danger.

Or **TRY BOTH!**

All we ask in return is that you answer 4 simple questions on the attached Treat Yourself survey. You'll get **Two Free Books** and **Two Mystery Gifts** from each series you try, *altogether worth over $20*! Who could pass up a deal like that?

Sincerely,

Pam Powers

Harlequin Reader Service

Treat Yourself to Free Books and Free Gifts.

Answer 4 fun questions and get rewarded.

**We love to connect with our readers!
Please tell us a little about you...**

◄ DETACH AND MAIL CARD TODAY! ▼

	YES	NO
1. I LOVE reading a good book.	○	○
2. I indulge and "treat" myself often.	○	○
3. I love getting FREE things.	○	○
4. Reading is one of my favorite activities.	○	○

TREAT YOURSELF • Pick your 2 Free Books...

Yes! Please send me my Free Books from each series I select and Free Mystery Gifts. I understand that I am under no obligation to buy anything, as explained on the back of this card.

Which do you prefer?

❏ **Love Inspired® Romance Larger-Print** 122/322 IDL GRDP
❏ **Love Inspired® Suspense Larger-Print** 107/307 IDL GRDP
❏ **Try Both** 122/322 & 107/307 IDL GRED

FIRST NAME   LAST NAME

ADDRESS

APT.#   CITY

STATE/PROV.   ZIP/POSTAL CODE

EMAIL ❏ Please check this box if you would like to receive newsletters and promotional emails from Harlequin Enterprises ULC and its affiliates. You can unsubscribe anytime.

LI/SLI-520-TY22

Jack's hand reached up and brushed her hair back. His touch was gentle, but she winced. "Ouch!"

He made a soft tsking sound. "That cut looks deep, and it's bleeding like mad. You might need stitches. The paramedics are going to have to check you out."

Jack didn't appear as if he had gotten hit as hard as she and Tanner had. The only blood on him was hers. It looked like he'd been through a fight and lost, not an explosion. He would probably walk away with a few bruises. She was glad. Her heart hurt thinking about Jack or Tanner being seriously injured, or worse.

Enough. She needed to distract herself. And him. Because Jack was still looking a bit panicky around the eyes. She ran a quick glance over his taut muscles and clenched teeth. Yep. Still revved up. She needed to get him to relax.

"You look better than the two of us," she joked, spinning her pointer finger between herself and Tanner.

He didn't laugh. Didn't even crack a smile. Instead, he locked his gaze on her and said, "I would have taken the full blast for you."

Whoa.

She wasn't ready to deal with something that intense.

Tanner groaned and keeled over.

Aghast, she forgot about her own injuries. Jack's arms dropped from her completely and they both surrounded Tanner, calling his name and trying to revive him. He didn't respond. She exchanged glances with Jack, concerned. Tanner's skin was pasty. When she reached out a hand to touch his face, it was clammy.

"Chief! Tanner's down!"

Chief Spencer abruptly cut his conversation short

and ran over. "What happened? He seemed fine a few moments ago."

"Shock, I think. Firefighters checked us out but thought we were okay to wait for the paramedics. We need to elevate his legs above his heart and get him warm."

Chief Spencer shrugged out of his jacket and bunched it up. "Roll him over on his back and put this under his feet."

He got on his radio and called for an ETA on the paramedics while Officer Beck grabbed a blanket from the back of one of the cruisers and raced over. He spread it out over the fallen special agent.

The chief sank down on his haunches beside Jack. "The paramedics are on their way. They should be here soon."

Nicole nodded. Small townships and boroughs like Sutter Springs didn't have their own ambulance service. They needed to wait for one from a larger city to arrive. It seemed to take forever, but it was only five minutes before the ambulance swerved to park along the side of the curb.

They tackled Tanner first, as basic triage said the most severe patient got immediate care. Nicole eased back to give them better access. She couldn't scoot too far away. When spots began to dance before her, Jack was suddenly there, his strong arm around her shoulders.

"Lean on me."

A second ambulance arrived. The paramedic emerged and spoke with the crew with Tanner.

She relaxed into his side, her head on his shoulder. He placed a soft kiss on her hair as they sat together and watched as the paramedics assessed Tanner. His vitals were taken. He didn't waken while they checked him out, although his pulse and blood pressure were good; they loaded him onto a gurney.

Nicole sat beside Jack, shifting into a slightly more comfortable position, as they watched the stretcher carrying his partner and friend's still form disappear into the ambulance. His arm stiffened around her. She tilted her head back to see his face. His stark expression wounded her. Catching her breath, she reached one hand up and wrapped her fingers around the hand hanging across her shoulders.

His fingers convulsed and gripped hers. She didn't mind the brief pain if it helped him. "He'll be fine," he whispered.

She wasn't sure if he was telling her or himself. "I'm sure he will be." She wanted to lean her head against his arm, to give him her strength.

"You're next." A paramedic popped into her vision. It was the one from the second ambulance.

She yelped, surprised. Jack's hand was still holding her own, keeping her anchored in place.

"My name's Bob. Do I have your permission to treat you?"

"Yes. Of course."

When Jack removed his arm so the paramedic could do his job, she missed it. She submitted to the paramedic's attention as graciously as she could. Impatience danced up her spine. She wanted answers.

Someone had planted a bomb in her car. A bomb. In her car. That stuff happened in movies, or in big cities. They did not happen in Sutter Springs. Although, Sutter Springs had been booming lately, thanks to the

growing tourist traffic through it. She frowned. Everyone wanted to know about the Amish. With so many
extra people in the town and surrounding area, it was
no wonder people like Brandon and Ted were able to
move around undetected. The police department sim-
ply did not have the manpower to keep track of it all.

"Has the bomb squad been called?"

"Yeah. They'll be here soon," Jack said. "Not sure
what they'll find. Your car is a mess."

"Thanks." Nicole grimaced.

"Any time. There will be a video of the parking lot."
Jack squeezed her hand. "Believe it or not, this may be
the big lead we needed. We might see the man who is responsible for all this. He wouldn't have known precisely
when you were going to be here, so it's possible he was
in the area to detonate the thing when you walked up to
the car. Maybe you'll recognize him in the flesh more
than you did in the picture Francesca drew."

"Maybe."

She wasn't convinced. Francesca was highly skilled.
She tried to recall the electrician who'd poisoned the
coffee earlier. All she really remembered was the way
he walked. But then, she'd never expected the electrician to be her attacker or that he'd get into the police
station itself.

He was bold, that was for sure.

The paramedic shone a light in her eyes, testing her
reflexes. She flinched back.

"Pupils look good. What's your name?"

"Nicole Dawson."

"Nice to meet you, Nicole. Tell me what happened.
Did you lose consciousness at all?"

"My car exploded." She shuddered. "I'm not sure how I was injured. I was unconscious for a time."

Furrowing her forehead, she glanced at Jack, silently begging him for help.

"You were hit by flying debris. You were out for about five minutes."

She blinked, surprised that she had been unconscious for so long.

The paramedic continued to ask her basic questions, testing her alertness. He also did a rapid injury assessment. "You don't appear to be hurt anywhere other than your head. However, you should have an X-ray to rule out other problems."

She didn't want to go. Nicole needed to know what happened to her car and see if she could remember the man who planted the bomb. If she went to the hospital, who knew how long she would be detained? It had been almost two full days since Leah disappeared and a day since Lucy was poisoned.

Nicole started to shake her head to protest. Unfortunately, the slight motion sent a wave of nausea swirling in the pit of her stomach. She gagged. Jack and the paramedic helped her reposition herself as she lost the contents of her stomach. Even then, completely hollow, the weakness and nauseous sensation persisted.

"Nicole, go to the hospital." Jack placed a tender kiss on her forehead. "I'll come and see you later. I will bring you all the information you need to know."

She could barely raise her head. "Jack…"

She wasn't positive what she wanted to say. *Thank you. I don't want to go. Don't leave me.* All those thoughts went through her mind. She couldn't say any of them. Instead, she allowed herself to be led and lifted into the ambulance. Her head ached. When the paramedic prompted her to lie down, she didn't argue. The prone position helped her stomach to settle.

The ambulance began to move. The gentle swaying motion lulled her into a light doze.

Jack stood and watched the ambulances carry his friend and the woman who was making strides in reclaiming his heart to the hospital. Tanner's unresponsiveness was especially disturbing. He'd gone down so fast. Jack scrubbed his hands over his face. He needed to get the information he promised Nicole, then he would be on his way to the hospital.

He bowed his head for a moment, thanking God that Nicole hadn't gone into the vehicle. That she had forgotten her bag. Otherwise...

He squeezed his eyes closed. He couldn't even think of the alternative. To consider a world without Nicole in it, regardless of whether they were together or not, was unbearable. Her presence was a light in his life.

Right now, though, he needed answers. The bomb squad was still talking with the chief. He walked over, casually inserting himself into the small group of law enforcement officers surrounding the newcomer. Beck and Zilhaver moved over to accommodate him, accepting his presence. The older man gave him a nod. Beck remained focused on the chief.

Jack had to admit—Officer Beck might be a rookie, but he was rising in his estimation, despite their initial rocky encounter. He would be a fine police officer.

"It was a homemade bomb," the man from the bomb squad was saying, pushing up his glasses with one hand and holding what was left of the device in his other. "It was triggered when the door was shut. It wasn't that well-made. If it had been, you—" he gestured to Jack "—would not have escaped without injury."

He made a few more comments regarding the composition and placement of the bomb. The chief thanked him for his time. Then he lifted his gaze to the camera stationed in the parking lot. Jack could almost feel the ice in that glance.

"I want to take a gander at the footage."

Jack stepped up beside him. "Mind if I tag along? I promised Nicole I would bring her answers."

"You don't need to justify it to me, Quinn. You and Special Agent Hall are part of this investigation. It's in my best interests to share all my resources with you." The chief started toward the entrance of the building. "Besides, I'm so angry, I'll take all the help offered to catch the person or persons responsible for injuring one of mine and your squad mate."

Jack nodded and set his own jaw. He understood the anger. It roiled in his gut, too.

Beck and Zilhaver joined them in the conference room. Together, the men sat in grim silence and watched the video of a man in a hoodie planting a bomb in Nicole's car. He swaggered around the car, arrogance in every motion.

"He's putting on a show," Jack spat, disgusted. "He doesn't care that the camera is there. In fact, I'd go as far as saying he *likes* being on camera."

"No, he doesn't seem to mind it at all. I'd agree with your assessment." Chief Spencer narrowed his gaze at the video. "Officer Beck, freeze it there."

The video paused when the man's face was visible.

"Get an image of this frame printed for the special

agent." He bit off each word and jerked a nod at Jack. "You can bring that to Sergeant Dawson when you go to visit her and Special Agent Hall. I think she'd want to see who put that explosive in her car."

"Appreciate it."

Officer Beck hurried from the room to get the image. When he returned, he handed it to Jack with the energy and intensity of an Olympic athlete passing a baton in a relay race.

The moment that picture touched his skin, Jack's heart pounded with an explosive rage. He had to clench his jaw and tighten his muscles to control it.

This man, whether his name was Brandon Hatnells or something else, would not get away with his reign of terror. He would not be allowed to continue to prey on children and pregnant women, or to kill those who got in his way.

Jack had not been able to save his sister. But he would not fail to save Nicole or Lucy. Or another woman who came to Brandon-whoever-he-was's attention. He was drawing a line in the sand, right now.

Clutching the image in his fist, Jack stalked out of the station and ran to his Escape. He jumped in and drove to the hospital, his fingers drumming on the steering wheel as he struggled with the strength of the anger and resolve filling his soul.

Romans 12:19 came to his mind. "Beloved, avenge not yourselves, but rather give place unto wrath: for it is written, Vengeance is mine; I will repay, saith the Lord."

A hard breath exploded from him. "Lord, I know that vengeance is Yours. Please help me to be just, not angry. I don't want to act outside of Your will. But I can't deal with this anger on my own."

A warm flood of peace spilled over him. The anger wasn't completely gone, but he could control it and do his job.

He arrived at the hospital and strode in, going immediately to the reception desk. He flashed his badge at the woman sitting behind the counter. "Can you give me the status on Special Agent Tanner Hall and Sergeant Nicole Dawson, please?"

After scrutinizing his badge and comparing the picture to his face, she nodded. "Yes, sir. Special Agent Hall and Sergeant Dawson are both in the ER. They have not been seen yet."

It might be a long evening. There were several other people in the ER, waiting their turn. Hopefully, they weren't too far behind and he'd be able to see them.

"Fine. Can you tell me the status of Lucy Hilty?"

"Lucy will be going home in the morning."

He hadn't heard about that. "Do you know where she's going?"

She glanced at him over her glasses, lips pursed. "All I know is she will be released at nine tomorrow. You'll have to talk with her or the doctor for more details."

Sighing, he walked away from the reception desk but didn't go near the waiting area. He needed privacy to call the station. Pulling out his phone, he dialed Chief Spencer's direct line.

"Chief, I'm at the hospital, still waiting to see our people. I checked on Lucy, and they're planning on sending her home tomorrow."

"Is that right?"

"Yes, that's what the receptionist said." Jack spun a

bit to make sure no one was close to him. "Sir, I don't feel she's ready to be in her home alone. She doesn't live with anyone else, and we know that she's a target."

The chief was silent for a moment or two. "I hear what you are saying, Quinn. I cannot promise you anything, but I will work on a solution. You don't worry about it, hear? I'll let you know what I figure out in the morning."

"It's a plan."

It was nearly two hours later when he was able to speak with Nicole. She was getting ready to leave, having been released.

"They didn't want to keep you overnight?"

She shrugged. "They did some tests and did an X-ray. I'm going home. I have some pain meds if I get a headache—"

"You probably won't fill the prescription."

She grinned at him. "I might, might not. I'm just thrilled to be going home. What have you found?"

He told her what they'd learned about the bomb and then showed her the image.

She scowled at it. "That's the guy from Fran's drawing, all right. The more I look at it the more certain I am that I know this man. I can't think where I saw him. But there's definitely something about him that rings a bell. I liked my car. And Tanner! This whole thing infuriates me." She handed the photo back, the corners of her mouth pulled down.

"It's frustrating. I get it." His fingers brushed hers as he took the image. He watched the flush steal into her cheeks. The urge to lean forward and kiss her lips made him step away. She was getting under his skin. "Listen, I know you'll argue, but as soon as I check in with Tanner, I'm going to drive you home. And I would like to sleep on your couch tonight."

He waited for it.

It didn't come.

"I think I'd like you to do that, too."

Shocked, he blinked. "I was sure I'd have a fight on my hands about that."

"Today really showed me how close he could get to me. Broad daylight and cameras didn't stop him. Even being at the police department didn't seem to make a difference. Jack, I accept your offer. My couch is yours. I'll even let you have access to my coffee maker. I don't want to be in that apartment by myself."

He left her for a few moments to look in on Tanner. His squad mate had been moved to a recovery room. He was propped up against the pillows, his expression annoyed and decidedly bored.

"What did the doctors say?"

Tanner grimaced. "I need to have a CAT scan. It's scheduled for first thing in the morning. They're concerned that I was unconscious for so long. I didn't come to until they brought me in to the emergency room."

Jack shook his head, frowning. "That doesn't sound good. How are you feeling?"

Tanner shrugged. "Never mind about me. Tell me what's been going on these past few hours."

Jack gave him a quick update. "Look. You get some rest. I'm sure you'll be back tomorrow."

"I hope." Tanner sighed and closed his eyes.

Waving goodbye, Jack went to find Nicole. She was waiting for him at the reception desk. He grabbed her hand and walked with her back to his car. Somehow, it felt natural to hold her hand in his. Almost like they were still a couple.

They didn't talk during the drive to her apartment. When they arrived, he plucked the red duffel bag he kept packed at all times from the back seat and followed her into the building. He was happy to see she had to use a special key to buzz herself in. They used the stairs to the second floor. Nicole didn't like elevators, he recalled.

Inside the apartment, they pulled out their guns and did a quick sweep through. When the apartment had been declared clear, Nicole went and gathered sheets, a blanket and a pillow and placed them on the arm of the couch.

"I appreciate you staying here." She yawned widely, her jaw cracking. "My, I'm ready to turn in."

"Oh." He recalled his conversation with the chief about Lucy and repeated it for her. "I don't have a clue what he'll come up with, but seriously, anything is better than having her stay in her home by herself."

She gave him a strange look.

"What?"

She shook her head. "I have an idea. Let me think about it, and I'll tell you tomorrow if it's something that might be workable."

His mouth slid open. Trust Nicole to drop something like that on a man, then leave, making him suffer with his own curiosity through the night.

TEN

It was a long night. Nicole tossed and turned, attuned to every creak and noise outside her room. She fluffed her pillow, slapping it a couple of times, and tried to get comfortable.

It didn't work. Her nerves were shot. She was too on edge. Her muscles were bunched up, and her legs felt like she needed to stretch them. After throwing back the covers, she paced the confines of her room for ten minutes, trying to work off the stress. Then she slipped back into her bed and resolutely closed her lids.

It was past four before she dropped off to sleep out of sheer exhaustion.

When her alarm went off at six, she smacked the snooze button twice before she managed to drag herself out of bed. She took her shower and dressed, then went to the kitchen to make herself a cup of coffee and breakfast. She passed through the living room on the way.

Jack was still asleep on the couch. She paused and stared down at him for a moment, tenderness for him stirring inside. She stretched out her hand but pulled it back before she could touch his hair.

She stepped away from him and continued to the kitchen. What she was feeling was impossible.

She bit her lip. What she was planning on doing smacked of hypocrisy. But it was the only way she could think of to protect Lucy until Brandon and Ted were caught. If the chief approved her idea. She had sent him a text about it the night before. He hadn't said yes or no. Before he could give her the go ahead, he needed to talk with Lucy's bishop. If Bishop Hershberger didn't agree, it would be a waste of time to discuss it.

Eventually, Jack woke up, said a sleepy good morning to her and retreated to the bathroom. In a few minutes, he sauntered into the kitchen, his hair wet from a shower, as she was scooping the cheesy eggs she had scrambled onto two plates. The bacon was ready, too.

"There's milk and juice in the fridge, or there's pods for the Keurig there." She gestured with the spatula to the K-Cup carousel on the counter. He slipped past her and spun the carousel.

"Morning blend, French vanilla, hot chocolate, caramel, deep roast... You sure do like your coffee, Nicole."

She snickered. "I have three other flavors in the cupboard, but I didn't have room to put them in it."

He laughed and plucked a morning-blend pod out and put it in the machine. Soon, the hearty aroma mingled with the scent of bacon in the air. He sat at the table and tucked into his breakfast.

When breakfast was over, he helped her clean up. Before they left for the station and got in his Escape, Jack walked around the SUV, looking under it and in all the crevices.

"Clear."

It wasn't until they were traveling that he brought up their conversation from the night before. "So? What's this brilliant idea you had?"

"Huh. Not so sure it's brilliant. But I do think it could work. The chief will tell us about it if it's a go."

He glared at her briefly. "You're not going to leave it there?"

"Yeah, I think I am."

She smirked, but her insides were quivering. She could see the parallels between what she was thinking of doing and what had broken them up. This experience was definitely helping her achieve a new perspective.

The chief called them into his office when they arrived. Nicole raised her eyebrows at the third chair in front of his desk. Normally, only two were stationed there. He waited until they were seated before he began speaking. "I have considered your idea, Sergeant, and I think it has possibilities. I've sent Beck to Bishop Hershberger's place. I would prefer to have the conversation here rather than in the community. I don't want anyone seeing you conversing with him like this."

Jack's brow furrowed.

Nicole pressed her damp hands down the front of her uniform slacks. Now that they were actually considering her idea, she wasn't sure it was a plausible strategy after all. Would she be able to pull it off? Would it put Lucy into more danger?

Before she could get too bogged down with her thoughts, someone knocked on the door. The chief called for them to enter. Officer Beck opened the door and ushered Bishop Hershberger inside.

Chief Spencer stood and held out his hand to shake the bishop's.

"Bishop Hershberger, thank you for joining us. Please, won't you sit down?"

The bishop settled himself into the third chair. "Chief

Spencer, I understand you have something to tell me, ain't so?"

"I do." The chief folded his hands on his desk. "Special Agent Quinn and Sergeant Dawson have told me that Lucy Hilty is scheduled to be released today. I believe she lives alone?"

The bishop tilted his head. "*Jah.* She is a widow. I have told the officers before that she would be more than welcome to stay in a number of other homes in our district."

The lines around the chief's mouth deepened.

Nicole clasped her hands over her knees, rocking slightly. What would they do if he didn't approve their plan? How would they protect Lucy while searching for Leah?

The chief cleared his throat. "Sergeant Dawson has a plan to protect Mrs. Hilty. Sergeant?"

Oh, she did not want to be the person explaining this. Especially not in front of Jack. How would he react?

"Well, I was thinking that Lucy has been through a traumatic event and really needs to return to her home. She has a new baby, and once he's ready to leave the hospital, she will need to be in her own house. And when we find Leah, she will do better in her familiar surroundings."

She drew in a deep breath. So far so good. Now she got to the tricky part. "I know that you have allowed a woman in Witness Protection to hide in your district. And I know that you've had undercover officers in your district before."

That was how she had met Kate Burkholder. Kate had been a police officer on an undercover mission in Sutter Springs. She had teamed up with Abram Burkholder, her childhood sweetheart. Now they were married with several children.

The bishop gazed at Jack, skepticism written all over him. "And what do you plan to do?" he asked, with that familiar lilting accent. "I do not think the agent would be able to hide in our district."

She smiled a bit, imagining Jack dressed Plain. "No, sir. Special Agent Quinn will not be going undercover. Just me."

Jack's eyes bulged. He straightened in his chair and stared at her.

The bishop leveled a serious stare on her. "You? What *gut* would it do?"

She knew she could not mention carrying a gun. "I can stand between Lucy and the attacker. If the men who are after her mistake me for Lucy, or come into her home, I can arrest them. The men we're searching for, they are not Amish, but they are going after pregnant Amish women. And we believe that they have targeted Lucy now because she saw them."

She leaned forward, begging him to see her point. "I want to bring them to justice. To keep them away from the Amish women and children they are targeting."

Bishop Hershberger ran his hand down his long beard and considered her argument. She held her breath. Finally, he came to a decision. "*Jah*. I will allow you to protect her. But I do not want you to use deadly force. You will try to do this without violence."

Jack couldn't believe the bishop had agreed to let her go undercover in the Amish district. When the bishop left, the chief and Nicole hammered out the details of the plan. Jack sat back, stunned.

He had heard what she had not spelled out for the bishop. She was going to be a decoy. This thought was verified when the chief mentioned making sure the colors of the dresses and aprons she wore while undercover matched those worn by Lucy.

Lucy and Nicole were not the same size. Lucy was a little shorter, but they were close enough that anyone who did not know them well might be fooled. She was risking her life, and the bishop was concerned that she might have a gun!

Although, she didn't promise not to use her gun.

At least she hadn't done that.

Still, the longer he thought about it, the more he was convinced it was a good plan. But that didn't mean he liked it. He hated it. Any possibility of her being abducted or hurt, or worse, was one that set his teeth on edge. Jack was smart enough not to voice his opinion in the chief's office. After all, he'd obviously thought sending Nicole undercover had merit.

Jack didn't say anything while Nicole and the chief finished up their conversation, consumed with his own thoughts.

"Special Agent Quinn?" Blinking, he stared at Nicole and Chief Spencer. He had clearly missed something.

"Sorry, sir. I was thinking. You were saying?"

The chief smiled, a quick quirk of his lips. "The drawings Francesca made have been disseminated to all the surrounding precincts. I want you two to spend a few hours spreading the photos of Leah around, talking to people and seeing if you get anywhere. By this afternoon, I should have what you'll need for your assignment, Sergeant."

Nicole avoided Jack's gaze. "What about Lucy? She's going home today."

"Don't you worry about her. I have assigned protection for her."

"But the bishop didn't want a police detail. That was the whole problem."

"And she's not getting one. Mrs. Hilty will be spending the day here with us. This evening, she'll go home, and you'll meet her there. Now, enough wasting time. I need you to make good progress this morning."

They were dismissed. As they walked out of the station and into the parking lot, Jack's mind returned to sifting through everything he'd heard in the past two days. There were still so many questions.

"Are you going to ignore me all day?"

He narrowed his eyes. "I'm not ignoring you. I wish you had shared your plan with me before we arrived. It wasn't fair to spring it on me like that."

"I didn't know if the chief would approve it."

Not much of an excuse. His car was parked on the other side of the lot. Shifting directions, they headed toward it. They were within ten feet when they heard a yell.

A man hurtled out of the bushes, charging straight at them. His white T-shirt was stained red near his shoulder. Another stain was spreading on his side. He slammed into the side of Jack's Escape, bounced off and collapsed on the ground.

Jack reacted on instinct, pushing Nicole behind him with one arm while reaching for his service weapon with the other. When the man on the ground groaned but made no other moves, he relaxed.

"It's Ted," Nicole breathed in his ear.

Jack replaced his gun in his holster and took a step toward Ted. He glanced back at Nicole. She had her weapon out and ready. Using the radio hooked to her shoulder, she called in a man down in the parking lot outside the station. When the dispatcher assured them someone was on the way, Nicole nodded, shifting her stance. She'd cover him if Ted moved suddenly. Jack crouched down beside the wounded man, wary.

"Ted? Can you hear me? Where are you hurt?"

Ted groaned again. He mumbled something.

"I didn't catch that. Ted? Say that again?"

With obvious effort, the wounded teenager opened his eyes. They were glassy with pain. "Shot. Twice." He moaned. "I didn't know. I wouldn't have done it if I'd known."

"Known what, son?" Jack didn't acknowledge Officer Beck when he made his way over to them. Beck was on his phone, apparently talking to dispatch. A theory confirmed when he murmured to Nicole that an ambulance was enroute.

Ted grimaced. "He said it was a way to make money. My kid sister needed surgery. No insurance. I didn't know he planned to steal babies. Or that he'd kill anyone."

"Does he still have that little girl with him?"

"Yes." The word was drawn out, ending in a pained hiss. "He is meeting her buyer in two days."

Jack stiffened. He filed that information away and returned to Ted's other statement. "Who did he kill, Ted?"

"Some guy, an electrician."

Zachary Fields.

"Did he kill anyone else, Ted? Any women?" Jack kept the anger from his voice, but it wasn't easy.

Ted frowned, his brow crinkled in thought. "I didn't see him kill any women. I think I heard him tell someone on the phone he had. But I didn't realize what he was talking about at the time."

Jack nodded, accepting the information. "Who was he talking to?"

"His dad."

Nicole sucked in a surprised breath. They had never thought that this was a family business.

"Did you ever hear his father's name?" Nicole's question was calm, but he sensed the rage behind it.

Ted never got the chance to reply. Bullets sprayed the parking lot. Officer Beck grabbed Ted under his arms and dragged him behind a cruiser for cover. Jack turned and whisked Nicole behind a second vehicle.

Shouts rang out from across the street as gunfire peppered the back of Jack's SUV. A bullet hit the back tire. A loud hiss erupted from it. The people on the sidewalk ran for cover. Two police officers dashed out of the police station, helmets and vests on, weapons out.

The shots stopped.

"Find where the sniper was shooting from." Nicole ordered and pushed herself out of Jack's arms. Before she stepped from behind the car, she scanned the area. Jack let her go. He crouched over and ran to the other side to check on Officer Beck and Ted. Beck was fine, his eyes huge in his pale face. Probably the first shooting he'd ever been in.

Ted, however, hadn't made it. His chest wasn't moving.

Jack saw the moment Beck realized the kid he'd tried to save was dead. His skin tightened and his throat convulsed with emotion.

Jack stooped down next to him. "You did well, Officer Beck. It's not your fault. Your first instinct was a good one. You put your life on the line for him. This is not your fault."

Officer Beck blinked up at him. "If I'd moved faster."

"He was severely injured when he came here." Nicole dropped down beside them. "Steve, look at me."

Officer Beck focused his gaze on Nicole.

"Ted had been shot at least twice before he found us. He had come to talk with us. Probably got shot because he was coming here. I don't think he would have made it. You did what you could."

Jack couldn't tell if the officer believed them, but what Nicole said was true. Ted had made a choice to come clean with the police. No matter how deep into trouble he'd gotten himself, he'd tried to make it right.

The coroner arrived. As he was wrapping up, Jack's phone rang. He pulled it out and glanced at it. Seeing Tanner's name, he answered. Jack was relieved when Tanner informed him he'd be fine. He was being kept overnight, but should be discharged sometime the next day.

Jack hung up, grateful his friend hadn't been hurt worse.

"Chief, do you want Jack and I to do the notification?" Nicole's soft voice interrupted his thoughts.

The family. Jack winced at the barely hidden pain in Nicole's voice. If the chief said yes, she would go and tell Ted's family with compassion, but she'd be hurting the whole time. He knew she'd tell him the family was hurting more. He had to admire her dedication and the strength of her character.

All the same, he hoped the chief would spare her. Jack would willingly go and do it himself if he could.

Not that it would be pleasant for him. Notifications had always left him raw.

"Actually, Chief, I'd like to request that assignment." Officer Beck clasped his hands behind his back and waited.

Chief Spencer put his hand on his officer's shoulder. "Granted, Beck. Take Hansen with you."

"Yes, sir."

"Everything's falling apart," Nicole said. "This whole case seems to be getting nowhere."

Jack didn't like the dejected note in her voice. Nicole was the strongest woman he'd ever known, always able to keep perspective. He had often wished he'd been blessed with more optimism.

"Not true. We have names. Lucy is alive. And we have pictures of Leah and Brandon, whoever he is."

"We should have more by now."

Jack reached out and grabbed her hand. "We'll get through this, Nicole. Just hold on to your faith."

She squeezed his hand. He pressed his lips together to stop the words he wanted to say. Words about how he would be by her side until they'd seen this case through.

He'd lost his chance with her long ago.

Now all he could do was help her solve this case and keep her safe.

There was no way he'd make it back to Columbus with his heart intact.

ELEVEN

Jack's car was part of the crime scene. There were at least two bullet holes in the back of it, and the tire was destroyed.

He didn't care about the vehicle, not really. It was a means of travel. Just a thing. What he did care about was that a life had been wasted.

"Jack." He looked at Nicole. She jingled her keys at him. "Let's take my cruiser. Since yours is out of commission."

"Might as well. I don't want to let any more time pass us by." He wanted to grab his travel mug but knew that wasn't feasible. "Let's stop and get coffee on the way."

They hopped into her cruiser. Nicole started the car, then dropped her hands to her lap. He waited. Nicole continued to sit. She played with her fingernails, biting her lip. Jack knew this posture well. Nicole was getting her thoughts together because there was something on her mind and she wasn't quite sure how to begin. She did this when she was feeling emotionally disturbed. Jack was pretty sure he knew what was swirling around her mind.

"You're thinking about Ted, aren't you?"

She raised her head and blinked. Her large brown eyes glistened with unshed tears.

His first instinct was to take her in his arms, but he resisted the impulse. Number one, they were in a police cruiser on duty. And number two, he no longer had the right to comfort her.

"He was just a kid, Jack. And that man, Brandon, played on his weakness. Made him into a criminal. That *boy*—" he heard the heavy emphasis on the word *boy* "—was in an impossible situation. He wanted to help his little sister."

Jack swallowed. His own sister had died because he'd been too late. Ted's sister might be alive, but she'd have to live forever with the knowledge that her brother died to help her.

"And then he killed him when he became a liability," Nicole finished.

Jack forgot his decision not to touch her and ran the edge of his knuckles down Nicole's cheek. "I know it's awful. I feel like someone kicked me in the gut when I think of what happened."

She nodded. "I don't think I'll ever get his face out of my head."

Some things you never forgot. They popped into your brain at odd moments or in the form of nightmares.

"We can't do anything for him, and for that I am sorry. We can get the man who is directly responsible for his death."

Her mouth firmed. She shifted the cruiser into Reverse and backed out of her space. "We can. Let's get started. I won't feel good until he's behind bars." She hit the brakes and shifted into Drive, pausing as she met his gaze. "I want to be the one to read him his rights and put the cuffs on him."

Their first stop was the post office. They talked with the customers and put pictures on the bulletin boards. No one recognized Leah or the perp they now referred to as Brandon. When they got to the local mall, however, they found someone who thought they had seen a man who looked like Brandon. They listened to his story, which wasn't much, just a vague notion he'd seen Brandon, then took all his contact information and told him they'd be in touch.

"If they saw Brandon in the area, maybe someone saw Leah."

They continued searching, knocking on doors and approaching people on the streets, without any success.

They were three townships to the west when a call came through.

2905 in progress...

"Kidnapping," Nicole whispered.

Jack held up a finger, then turned up the volume. The dispatcher's message chilled him through and through. His gut clenched like he'd swallowed a lead balloon. Not only a kidnapping, but a pregnant Amish woman had been taken in the middle of the day from an Amish-run restaurant. The boldness was unbelievable. His fellow agents would never believe that the same kidnapper who planned his attacks so carefully would grab a woman in such a public venue.

"He's getting careless."

Nicole shook her head. Her dark ponytail swung over her shoulder. "I don't think it's carelessness. At least, not completely. I think he's getting desperate. Maybe he's in a bind, like he has a client on the hook for the baby."

Jack put the call into the station. "We're on our way, sir."

"I'll notify the local authorities so they'll know you're coming and why."

The restaurant parking lot was overflowing. In fact, there were more vehicles than customers, it looked like. Cars and buggies filled every spot and were lined up along the road. Several vehicles had television and radio station logos on them. Row upon row of people meandered about, the onlookers craning their necks or standing on tiptoe to get a better view of the drama unfolding.

The police vehicles on the scene were blocking the exit of the parking lot, lights flashing, splashing blue and red beams on the buildings, vehicles and spectators.

Nicole parked on the side of the road with the other vehicles, and she and Jack got out and headed to the restaurant. They had to pass close by a news crew setting up their equipment. The newswoman caught a look at Nicole's uniform and ran over to her.

"Officer, would you be available to comment—"

Nicole narrowed her gaze. "Sorry. I have no comment."

She ducked her head and strode past the woman. Jack picked up his pace, ignoring her calls. He had seen the camera rolling. He would not be surprised to see Nicole and him on the evening news, or at least their backs as they escaped the bold journalist.

Inside the restaurant, the staff was milling around, attempting to calm the anxious guests. Cameras were flashing and police were working the scene, interviewing customers and employees. Jack and Nicole made their way through the crowd and into the kitchen. The noise level there was even worse. Ignoring the chaos, they walked directly to the back door, which opened onto a narrow brick alley.

After stepping out, they spent a few minutes looking around for hints of a struggle.

"He took her here."

Nicole and Jack whirled around to find a young girl, maybe twelve or thirteen, standing uncertainly by the door. Her dark green dress and apron, along with her simple white *kapp*, identified her as Amish.

Nicole moved away from the open door. Jack hung back, giving them some space. The poor kid looked nervous enough to bolt if they spoke too loudly. He had to give her props for speaking to them at all. It showed a lot of courage, speaking to English officers after seeing a woman kidnapped.

"You saw it happen?" Nicole's voice was perfect, low and gentle.

The girl nodded. "*Jah.* Martha wasn't feeling well. Sometimes she needs to step outside for air."

"You were with her."

"She is my sister." Her blue eyes blinked. A single tear ran down her cheek.

"What's your name?"

"Addie. I always go with her. So she's not alone."

Jack stepped up cautiously. Martha gave him a skittish glance but didn't move. His admiration for her deepened. He kept his voice as quiet as he could, the same way he'd talk with a wounded animal.

"Addie, can you tell us what happened? Please?"

"*Jah.*" Addie breathed in deep. She appeared to be fortifying herself for the retelling. Nicole and Jack both remained still, giving her time. "Martha started feeling warm at dinner. *Mamm* told me to *cumme* with her. We stood out here for a few minutes. She was thirsty and asked me to get her some water. I ran in and got it. When I came out, a man was pushing her into a car. I dropped the glass." She pointed at the shattered fragments on the bricks. "I ran after the car, but they turned and I couldn't catch up."

Poor kid, Jack thought.

Nicole reached into the bag on her shoulder. "Do you recognize this man?" She showed her the picture of Brandon.

Addie's gaze grew wide. "*Jah!* That's the man who took my sister. Do you know where she is?"

"We will do our best to find her, Addie." Nicole smiled at her. "You have helped us a lot. We're going to share what you said with the other police here, okay?"

She nodded. "*Jah*. I can go now?"

Jack told her yes. He knew it was pointless to detain her against her family's wishes. "But tell your parents you might have to talk to the police again."

He could guarantee it. She ran back inside to her family. Jack and Nicole followed her and asked for the person in charge. They were directed to a tall woman with an imposing manner. They approached respectfully and waited for her to acknowledge them.

"You must be Sergeant Dawson and Special Agent Quinn." She held out a hand to them. "I'm Chief Morrow. Your chief, Spencer, informed me that we have a common enemy."

"Yes, ma'am." Nicole gave her a brief history of their case up to that point. "Chief, we just met a young girl in the back alley who told us the missing woman is her sister. She witnessed the kidnapping."

Chief Morrow snapped to attention. "Lieutenant Val!"

A hawk-faced police officer appeared at her side.

"Where's the little girl who saw the kidnapping?" she rapped out. Lieutenant Val's posture stiffened. When they pointed the child out, he hurried to where she sat with her family.

Jack had always heard that Amish people didn't like to talk with police. Martha's family, however, talked with them easily. The grief and anxiety were coming off her parents in waves.

Jack had briefly worried that he and Nicole would be kept on the outside of the search. He was wrong. Instead of being treated as interlopers, they were included in the search efforts for Martha Troyer, age twenty-three and seven and a half months pregnant. After receiving their directions, they piled back into Nicole's cruiser and took the route that the chief outlined for them, searching for the car, Martha or Brandon or anything suspicious.

They had just stopped at a stop sign when Nicole gasped and pointed. "Look there!"

A very pregnant Amish woman staggered down the road, her *kapp* askew, her face a mask of fear, covered with scratches.

Nicole jumped out of her cruiser and slammed the door, vaguely aware that Jack was doing the same on the passenger side. Glancing both ways for traffic, she sprinted after the young woman, calling her name.

"Martha! Martha Troyer, wait!"

Martha obviously wasn't prepared to stop for anyone.

In her present state, it didn't take more than a couple of minutes to overtake her. She hit out in an anguished frenzy when they appeared in front of her.

Nicole waved her hand low, silently telling Jack to stand down. He backed up, his posture tense like a stretched rubber band ready to snap in case he needed to jump into action. Hopefully, he wouldn't have to. But Martha's head kept jerking between them, her breath escaping in harsh gasps.

Martha whimpered. The animal sound ate at Nicole's heart. No one, ever, should sound like that. The surge of rage was so intense, for the space of two full seconds, Nicole literally could not see what was in front of her. Only her training and years of experience kept it under control.

She pushed past the fury and concentrated on the safety and well-being of the woman before her.

"Martha, you're safe now. You're all right." Nicole inched closer, her hands up and open. "I'm Sergeant Nicole Dawson. Your family called in the police. We've been searching for you."

No response.

"Martha, Addie is worried about you."

"Addie?" The first layer of fear began to clear. "You have talked with Addie?"

Nicole moved closer. Martha, still skittish, backed away. Nicole stopped. The last thing she wanted to do was to frighten the young woman back into her captor's path.

"Yes, we have talked to Addie. She watched you being taken and ran after the car."

That seemed to shake Martha from her overwhelming fear. A spark of anger flushed her pale face. "*Ack!*

What did she think she was doing? To put herself in danger! She is *gut*, *jah*?"

Nicole made a calming gesture with her open hands. "She's fine. Rattled, and very worried about you. But no harm came to her."

She scanned the scratches on Martha's face. "I'm guessing those scratches are from when you escaped."

Martha gave a single vigorous nod. "*Jah*. The man who took me brought me to a *haus*. Another man was there—I think it was his father. He was angry and they were yelling at each other. The older man, the father, was upset that the other hadn't taken care of someone named Lucy."

She paused. "Maybe he had a sister or a girlfriend who was sick?"

Nicole didn't want to tell her that taking care of Lucy meant killing her. "Maybe. How did you get away from them?"

The pregnant woman shuddered and wrapped her arms around herself as if she were freezing. It was nearly eighty degrees outside in the shade.

"They didn't check the back door. It was open. Just a little. I didn't see it at first, but when I looked at the door again, it wasn't flush with the wall. I snuck out while they were arguing. I was so scared. I didn't know what they'd do to me if they caught me again."

"You were very brave, Martha." Jack stayed back when he made the comment.

Martha shrugged. "I don't know if I was brave. I was scared and I wanted to go home. I want to go home to my Jacob."

Jacob must have been her husband.

"We'll get you home, Martha. But first, would it be

all right if we called the police and had someone meet us at your home? We're not the law enforcement in your area. We're only helping."

Martha opened her mouth and it looked like she might protest additional police.

Jack broke in. This time he did step forward. "Please, Martha. These men, they are taking women from Amish communities. Separating mothers and children. It has to stop."

Placing a protective hand over her stomach, Martha finally nodded, drooping with exhaustion. "*Jah*. I will agree."

"Thank you."

"Please, I want to go home now."

Jack and Nicole led her back to the cruiser. Jack opened the front passenger door and gestured for her to get in. He hopped into the back seat. Nicole bit back a grin at Jack sitting in the back, where criminals would normally sit.

She got in and buckled up and did a clean three-point turn on the road. She steered the car in the direction of town. A motor roaring up from behind had her glancing in her mirror.

She saw the gun a moment before the first bullet hit the bumper. "Get down!"

Martha shrieked and hunched in her seat, her pregnancy making it difficult to get any lower.

Nicole swerved on the road, riding the center of the road so the car behind her couldn't move up beside her. There were vehicles ahead. She needed to keep in his way so he didn't shoot a civilian. If only she could better protect Martha.

"Roll down the back window!"

Nicole jabbed the button with her finger and heard the familiar hiss as the window lowered. It stopped at the midpoint, but Jack didn't hesitate. Getting close to the window, he extended his weapon out and took two quick shots.

The first shot knocked out the side mirror. The second hit the rearview mirror.

The vehicle never slowed down. It continued to barrel toward them.

Nicole got on the radio and demanded to speak with Chief Morrow. "This is Sergeant Dawson," she yelled. "We have Martha Troyer in my cruiser and are being pursued. Our pursuer has a weapon and is taking shots."

"Sergeant, what is your location?"

She gave the number of the interstate highway. "Hold on… We just passed mile marker 152, heading east. Martha escaped her captors near here, so their hideaway could be nearby."

"There's a turnaround a mile ahead. Take that. I have officers en route to intercept."

Nicole saw the turnaround soon after. Without using her blinker, she swerved across both lanes and careened into the turnaround, doing a quick U-turn to head west on the interstate. Horns blared beside her as the blue car chasing her followed suit.

Less than a mile down the road, she heard sirens and saw lights flashing behind her, coming up fast.

Brandon, or whoever was driving the car, must have seen them, too. He shot across the road and bounced onto an exit, nearly veering into the side of an 18-wheeler. He swooped around the big truck and kept going. The sirens continued to flash as two of the cruisers took off after the blue car. The remaining cruiser kept pace with Nicole.

When the phone rang, she picked it up. "Sergeant, my officers said they are in pursuit. Are you out of danger?"

"For the moment, Chief."

"And Mrs. Troyer?"

Nicole cast an assessing glance at the young woman, trembling in the passenger seat. "She's shaken up, but other than that, she's well. Where would you like me to take her?"

"Bring her into our station. She'll need to make a report, and she should have a medical checkup—"

"Nee," Martha burst out. "I am fine. I do not need to see a doctor. I want to see my husband. I need to see Jacob."

The chief altered her instructions. "You will, Mrs. Troyer. I will personally make sure your family and husband are brought to the station. They will meet you here. We will have to discuss your safety after that."

Martha's lips grew taut, but she didn't argue.

At the station, they waited for Jacob Troyer to be brought in before they talked with his wife. When he arrived, he sat patiently as Nicole showed Martha the image of Brandon. The young woman shuddered and buried her face in her hands. Her husband looped an arm around her shoulders, his face fierce.

"That's him," Martha said, her words muffled. "That is the man who kidnapped me."

She swiped her apron across her face, wiping away the tears, and faced them. "Who is he and why did he take me?"

This was the part Nicole dreaded. As gently as she could, she related the parts that were relevant to Martha. When the woman gasped and buried her head in Jacob's shoulder, Nicole had the sudden urge to reach back and grab Jack's hand. She ignored the temptation. She didn't need his support, had gotten along fine without it.

When his hand casually dropped onto her shoulder, warmth drizzled through her.

When this case was over and he returned home, she'd have an uphill battle getting used to not having him around.

TWELVE

It was after four by the time they arrived back at her own Sutter Springs Police Department. Nicole hadn't been this exhausted since her last thirty-six-hour duty shift. Those were rare, but they did happen.

When she approached her desk, she sighed as she saw the paper bag with the rope handles sitting on top of her laptop. She knew what was in the bag. She regretted her suggestion, but it was too late now.

How would she fool anyone into believing she was Amish, even for a short time? She'd been a cop for so long, it was ingrained in her. She talked like a cop, reacted like one. Calling the image of Lucy to mind, she didn't see herself as capable of creating the illusion of being her.

With a heavy sigh, she hooked the bag around her fingers and hefted it off the desk.

"Going to change into your cover?" Jack asked.

She nodded, making a face. "It sounded so much more reasonable when I suggested it. Now I doubt it will work."

He placed a knuckle under her chin and gently nudged her face up. Reluctantly, she met his gaze. There was no mockery there. No sign that he wanted to say, "I told you so." Rather, his lips twitched up in an encouraging smile. "You can do anything, Nicole. I firmly believe that."

When he leaned over and kissed her, she held her breath. "I believe in you."

The brief contact had barely counted as a kiss. His lips had been there and gone, featherlight, before she could react. Her pulse kicked up and her breath caught. If a little kiss did that, a real one would do her in.

She backed away and nearly ran to the locker room to change. The dress was softer than she'd expected, although she twitched her shoulders, trying to get used to the feel of the strange garment. And the sleeves. Nicole always wore short sleeves in the summer, but those of the dark blue dress she donned came nearly to her wrists.

The other thing she had trouble wrapping her mind around was that her dress had no pockets. Where was she supposed to carry her cell phone and her gun?

Then she lifted the apron and relaxed. Her chief was a man of vision. He'd enclosed a small piece of fabric sewn up like a pocket and several large safety pins. She inspected it and smiled. She could attach it to the dress under the cover of the apron. It was big enough to carry the two items she needed and not much else.

If she had to get to the weapon in a hurry, it might be cumbersome, but she had no other options. She shrugged the worry off. She would have to be careful and keep her eyes peeled. Next, she had to put her hair up. Did Amish women wear buns? Twists? Braids? She had no idea. The question had never occurred to her before.

For the time being, she braided her long hair and used the pins included to secure it on the back of her head.

Finally, she lifted the starched white prayer *kapp* from the bag. Up close, she realized the tiny piece of fabric was much more elaborate than she'd imagined. It was perfectly round on the back, almost like a teacup. The cap shape was created with small, perfectly spaced pleats. There had to be over fifty of them!

Nicole was able to hem a skirt or a pair of pants. She could replace a button and even do a neat running stitch, thanks to her home economics teacher. That was the limit of her sewing and crafting abilities. She was fascinated by the quality and workmanship she found in a simple Amish *kapp*.

Finally, she pulled on heavy black stockings and boots to complete the outfit. She'd been in the locker room too long. Shoving the *kapp* on her head, she walked back to her desk, flushing when she passed a couple of her more seasoned colleagues. Thankfully, no one made any comments.

Jack grinned when he saw her.

"What's so funny?" She narrowed her eyes, daring him to laugh.

"Nothing." He shook his head. "Do you know, I don't think I've ever seen you in a dress?"

"That can't be right."

"Not once. Every time I've taken you out, you wore slacks."

The innocent reminder of what they'd once been to each other was the equivalent of having a bucket of cold water splashed on them. The smiles slid off both their faces. The longing to step closer to him was overwhelming.

She pivoted away and started walking to the door. "Coming, Special Agent Quinn? We need to get Lucy and bring her back to her place."

She heard his hard-soled shoes clumping up fast behind her but didn't turn around. She had almost made a big mistake there. She'd forgotten that they were no longer together, and for a few brief moments had enjoyed the camaraderie that had so marked their relationship before he began his work with the FBI.

Shoving open the station doors, she instinctively swerved to head to her cruiser. Jack caught her hand. The warm tingles shooting up her arm were an unhappy reminder of what she couldn't have.

She pulled away and looked at him.

He shoved his hands in his pockets, confusion darkening his brow. "I think we should take my car. It has some bullet holes, but the tire's been replaced, so it's good to go. It would look odd for an Amish woman to be driving a police vehicle."

"Duh. I wasn't thinking." Keeping the distance between them, she walked to his car. When he opened the door for her, she was very careful to avoid any contact.

She could sense his hurt but couldn't help it. The feelings they had for each other were hopeless. She needed to protect herself.

She understood a bit about how torn he would feel, her playing a part. But her fear was real. What if he played a role so often it became real?

She would never put herself into the position her mother had, of never knowing if her husband was lying or telling the truth. Regardless of whether it was necessary for his job or not, the ability to keep secrets well enough to fool experts was not one she wanted in a spouse. She couldn't handle having the man she loved keeping secrets from her.

And she did love Jack Quinn. Just as much now as she had three years ago.

Love didn't matter, though. She was still going to have to let him go when the time came.

What had caused Nicole to withdraw so quickly? One minute they were sharing a smile, and the next, she treated him like a stranger. The memory of how she'd removed her hand from his, her expression remote, flashed through his brain. It had hurt, he wouldn't deny it.

He knew she'd felt the same connection he'd been feeling for the past two days. The dazed look on her face after he'd kissed her so impulsively earlier was all the proof he needed. She had wanted to kiss him back, too. Before she'd run to the locker room.

Stop! This had to stop. He had no business getting involved with his ex-fiancée again. The issues that had torn them apart in the first place were still at play. In fact, he couldn't see a time in the near future when they wouldn't be.

It was a situation without a solution. He needed to remember his purpose for this visit. The moment this case was solved, he was heading home. If the case continued too long, he might have to leave Tanner in charge— once he was discharged from the hospital, of course. It wasn't good for Jack to be away from Chloe for too long.

Nicole had done the right thing, reminding him that they were colleagues, professionals working on a joint case, and nothing more. He rubbed the dull ache in his chest, trying to ignore the reason for it.

Lucy was waiting for them at the bishop's house when they arrived. They spent a few awkward minutes talking with him. He was kind, but Jack could see how careful Nicole was being, trying not to say anything that might cause him to change his mind about letting her stay with Lucy.

After ten minutes, they collected Lucy and left. She was holding Leah's doll in her arms. Jack had to look away. It saddened him knowing that in her own way, she was trying to hold her children close to her heart.

Her son, she explained, was still in the hospital. Jack had already known that, but he didn't interrupt the concerned mother as she told them that her little boy, Andrew, would be in the hospital for another week or so.

"He was born too early. His lungs aren't ready to breathe on their own yet."

He heard the pain. She was trying to be strong. But she was so young, and her entire family was dead, missing or in the hospital. It seemed harsh to bring her to an empty house.

"Lucy, are you sure you want to go home?" Nicole asked suddenly, echoing his thoughts. "We could bring you somewhere else."

"*Nee.* My two older sisters live nearby. I do not want to bother them. They all have families of their own. Besides, Naomi and Rose are involved in the tourist events. I don't want to be involved in that right now. I want to go home, where it's quiet and I can think."

Nicole didn't persist. The rest of the journey was made in silence. When they finally arrived at the house, Lucy gasped.

The front door was wide open.

THIRTEEN

Nicole jumped out the car almost before Jack shifted into Park. She removed the gun she'd concealed in the dress, and between the two of them, they canvassed the entire house.

Lucy cried upon entering her home and seeing the mess that had been made. While the place hadn't been completely trashed, it was clear someone had been inside and had deliberately vandalized her home.

Nicole met Jack in the kitchen. She winced as Lucy's sobs carried in from the living room. "The upstairs hasn't been touched. And there are no drawers upended or papers messed with."

Jack leaned his head closer. "I checked in the barn and the perimeter. Same thing. No one is in there, nor does anything appear disturbed."

"They didn't come to look for something." Nicole scanned the kitchen, tracking the shattered dishes and the glass fragments on the floor. "All the damage is surface. He was here for the sole purpose of frightening that poor woman."

Jack snorted, scorn in the curl of his lip. "A mean trick, that. He's escalating. Why waste time on something like this? I don't know if he's feeling overconfident or if his father's anger is making him careless. What I do know is that he's more dangerous now than he was two days ago. He's going to be taking risks, and his temper is shot."

She nodded, her stomach sinking. She'd had the same thought when she'd seen the pristine second floor.

She lowered her voice. "I don't think I'll be able to convince her to leave, although I will try. I don't like her here. She's been through so much. However, we do have the advantage of her knowing the house better than him. After she settles down, she and I are going to seek out a place she can hide, just in case."

"I don't think you'll convince her, either. I can stay—"

She shook her head. "If he sees your car here, he'll never come near me. I want him to come where we control the place. This may be our best opportunity to catch him, and you know it. He's obsessed with taking care of these loose ends. I'm one. Lucy's one."

His face told her he knew it but didn't like it. That was too bad. While his concern touched her, she needed to do her job. Sometimes that put her at risk, but she'd known that when she accepted the position. It was too late to back out. People were counting on her. Lucy. Leah. And any other pregnant Amish woman whom Brandon might come across.

"I know," he admitted. "Lock the doors when I leave. Keep your phone on at all times. And call me immediately if you need me."

She nodded, unable to speak over the lump clogging her throat.

When he leaned down and kissed her, she forgot her promise to keep her distance and kissed him back.

He lifted his head and touched her cheek with his hand. Then he pivoted on his heel and left. A minute later, she heard his car driving off.

She shook herself free of the fog his kiss had put her in and strode to where Lucy sat in the living room. "Lucy, let's find you a place to hide."

Lucy startled. "Hide?"

"Yes. If he comes back here, I want you to have a safe place to go. I'll deal with him."

The Amish woman looked doubtful, but she nodded and moved slowly upstairs, which reminded Nicole that she had recently had surgery.

"I'm sorry. Should you be climbing stairs?"

"*Ach.* This was my second C-section. I barely feel it."

Scar tissue. Hmm. Still, she didn't want to over-work Lucy.

Once they were upstairs, Lucy showed her around the possible places to hide. None of them were exactly what she'd had in mind, but given the circumstances, she agreed that if needed, Lucy could hide on the stairs that led to the attic. They were tucked behind a small door that was barely visible, disguised behind a large rocking chair covered with a handmade quilt.

Nicole turned on the propane fueled stove and heated up some dinner the bishop's wife had sent with them, but Lucy didn't have much of an appetite. Nicole put the leftovers in the fridge, and Lucy announced she was heading to bed. Nicole wandered the main floor, prowling from room to room and peering out windows.

She was tired, but her nerves were keyed up. She'd never get to sleep knowing that Brandon was out there bent on harming Lucy and her.

Around eleven thirty, her instincts were proven correct. She was in the living room when she heard soft steps on the back porch. He was trying to tread quietly.

Heart pounding, she slipped upstairs and into Lucy's room.

"What?" Lucy came awake almost instantly. She hadn't been in a deep sleep.

"Hide."

Jack hadn't returned to the hotel. The idea of leaving those two women out here alone was the epitome of wrong, in his humble opinion. The chief had agreed and had ordered another officer to help him keep watch. He drove his car a mile up the road and left it parked in an abandoned church lot. He would wait out the entire night if he had to and rest in the morning.

When Officer Beck arrived, they decided to take turns keeping watch. Turning his head, he saw the rookie snoring in his car.

Jack smiled, then reached for his phone when it pinged.

His blood froze.

He's here

Brandon had shown up. Smacking his horn, he watched as Beck jerked awake at the short blast. He held up his phone and pointed down the road. Beck immediately started his cruiser.

Smart kid.

They drove to the Hilty place and left their vehicles on the road. Jack pointed, indicating for Beck to go around the house to the back. He nodded and disappeared. Jack crossed to the front stairs. A gun went off. Jack tore open the door as a man yelled in the next room. Glass shattered. Snatching his flashlight from his belt, he ran into the other room. The man had smashed open the back door so hard the window had broken. Streaks of blood covered the floor.

He heard Beck shout "Police! Halt!"

A minute later, a motorcycle fired up. Beck's cruiser pulled out after him.

Nicole ran to the door.

"Nicole!"

She spun to see him. "I'm fine. We're both fine. He had a gun and shot at me, but missed. I think I nicked his arm. Not sure. It was dark in here."

She left to check on Lucy. When she returned, she slid into a chair and rested her head against the back-rest. "Lucy has agreed to move in with her sister tomorrow morning. I think we need to hit the streets at first light and start going door-to-door searching. We know Brandon is in the area. That means Leah might be, too."

FOURTEEN

Breakfast was a quiet affair the next morning. Nicole didn't talk as she served them efficiently. Jack nodded when she caught his eye and frowned in the Amish woman's direction. Lucy's face was pale and dark purple smudges had formed under her eyes. Jack was fairly sure that she was too exhausted for conversation. Plus, he doubted anyone slept well in the house after the break-in the night before.

Officer Beck helped her stand, compassion gleaming in his eyes. "Mrs. Hilty, why don't we swing by the hospital this morning before going to your sister's house? You can look in on little Andrew."

She smiled at him, a wobbly little quirk of her lips, and thanked him in her quiet way.

Jack walked them out to the car, uneasy in light of what had happened the night before. Brandon had taken his motorcycle off road and had not been seen since. Beck, he knew, blamed himself for letting the man get away.

"You couldn't have done anything," Jack said. "He was able to travel where you couldn't."

The fact that it had been pitch-dark out hadn't helped. If only it hadn't been a new moon, the sky black. If...

It was useless trying to change what had happened.

"When you get to the hospital," he murmured to Beck, "check if anyone matching Brandon's description with a gunshot wound in his arm has been there."

The hospital had to report such things, but if the report hadn't been filed yet, Beck would find out.

As Nicole had suggested, she and Jack took the pictures of Brandon and Leah and headed out. Nicole hadn't brought a uniform with her, so she was still dressed in her Amish outfit. In the yard, Nicole stopped. She bent down and retrieved Leah's doll.

"It must have fallen." The sorrow in her voice lanced through him.

Jack took two steps to her side and gave her a hug, kissing the top of her head. "We will do all we can." How he wished he could promise success. But he couldn't and Nicole knew it.

She pulled away so she could look up into his eyes. "I know we will. But sometimes all we can do is not enough."

She touched his face, then stumbled out of his arms and got into the car, the doll still clutched in her hand.

She hadn't been talking about Leah or their case. His heart was bleeding inside as he opened his door and got into the car. He wanted to scream at the universe. *Why?* He and Nicole belonged together, except she refused to trust him.

"Why, Nicole?" he burst out. He hadn't planned on saying anything, but the pain wouldn't let him keep silent.

She licked her lips. "Jack. You have to know I'm proud of you. You are an incredible man. A great cop and agent."

"But?"

She sighed. "It's really a case of 'it's not you, it's me.' My dad, he was a consummate liar. And unfaithful to my mom. Many times. He was a skilled liar. And she believed him. When she found out the extent of his deceit after his death, it nearly destroyed her."

Each word hit his battered heart like a hammer.

"She shut me out. I had lost my dad, and then my mom emotionally abandoned me, turning to drinking. Even before she died, I was an orphan."

"You can't believe I'm like that. That I would do such a thing to you."

She shook her head. "No. I don't. And I know this sounds weak because I'm undercover, so to speak, right now. But I already know I will not ask for this kind of assignment again. I have seen what happens to someone who goes on undercover operations, the dark places where you go. Lying becomes a habit. I wouldn't know when you weren't telling the truth. And that would eat at me. So, while I trust you, somewhere in my mind I would always wonder. It would kill anything we tried to build."

"I'll give it up."

She turned to him, her mouth dropping open. "I would never ask it of you."

There was nothing else to be said. They spent their morning going from door to door. They knocked on Amish and non-Amish doors alike. One hour passed. Then another. His stomach growled. Still they continued, desperation urging them on. Leah had been gone three days now.

Had she been sold to someone else? Or did Brandon still have her with him? It was a chilling thought. One which, by silent agreement, they refused to talk about. Until they knew for sure, they would try to keep hoping.

Hope became harder every time someone told them "Sorry, but I haven't seen them."

It was around noon when they had approached the Plain and Simple Bed and Breakfast. The owner of the place, Dean Burkholder, took one look at the picture of Brandon and his eyes widened. "I think I've seen this man. Adele!"

A pretty young woman came into the room. She smiled at them, but then she saw Nicole and her gaze widened. "Sergeant Dawson!"

Jack kept his mouth from falling open. "You've met?"

"Adele Burkholder. Of course." Nicole smiled. "We met several years ago at her cousin Abram's wedding."

"Adele King now."

Quickly, after explaining why Nicole was in Amish garb, they showed her the picture of Brandon and Leah. "I know Lucy and her daughter. She's one of my best friends." Adele frowned. "This man. It seems to me that I have seen him. I don't recall his name, but he was here before."

"I'll tell you what," Dean said. "Adele here needs to return to her *haus*, but I will show his picture around to the other guests. And if anyone recognizes him, I'll have them call you."

They nodded and Jack gave them his cell phone number.

Adele removed her work apron and hurried out the door. That's when Jack noticed it. She was pregnant.

Jack's mind flashed to Andrew and the missing Leah. He'd never thought how vulnerable children were. Not until recently.

If he had time, he'd call up Joyce right now and ask about Chloe. Funny how much he needed to know that his niece, his little girl, was fine. He would call her the first opportunity he got. Right now, he had a case to solve.

"Did you notice that she was pregnant?" Nicole chewed on her knuckle, disturbed. "If Brandon stayed there at the Plain and Simple Bed and Breakfast, he would have seen her and noticed that."

Jack started the car. "I did notice. I have a feeling this case is about to bust wide open. I don't know how we can insist on protection for Adele King, but we should try. Can you call the chief?"

She nodded, pulled out her cell and was on with her boss in a few seconds, asking for a guard for Adele.

"I don't know, Sergeant. You say there's been no direct threat made against her?" The chief's voice boomed into the car on speaker.

"She did say Brandon looked familiar."

"Lots of people look familiar. We're short-staffed right now tracking down leads. I'll do what I can, but it might mean we just have a cruiser go by now and then."

"Thanks, Chief." She disconnected and huffed out a breath as she bumped her head lightly against the headrest.

Jack gave her an encouraging smile. "If I had my

druthers, we'd put all the pregnant women under guard until Brandon and his gang were no longer a threat."

Her eyes narrowed. "You know, once we find him, we already have a lead on who's calling the shots."

He nodded. "I thought about that. His father. If Martha was correct."

"If," she agreed. "It would make life easier, for sure."

His stomach gurgled. "I can't take it anymore. Let's get something to eat before we head out again."

They hit a small ice cream hut right around the corner from the police station that sold burgers and sandwiches. Not exactly health food, but it was quick and tasted good. Nicole ordered a salad with crispy chicken, and he had a cheeseburger with bacon on it. Neither took the time for ice cream.

"I can't afford it anyway," Nicole said when he asked if she minded forgoing dessert. "I've eaten way too much sugary stuff."

He should have thought of that. "I'm sorry. I should have found somewhere else."

She tapped his arm. "Stop. This is fine. I have a salad with chicken and hard-boiled eggs. So what if the chicken was fried? I still got my protein."

His phone rang as they returned to the car. He answered as he opened the doors and immediately put it on speaker.

"Hello? Special Agent Jack Quinn. How can I help you?"

"Um, yeah, um, my name is Darcy Taylor. I was given this number…" Her voice trailed off.

Even through the phone, Nicole could sense the woman's discomfort. Would it help if she were talking to a woman?

Acting on instinct, Nicole broke in. "Ms. Taylor? My name is Sergeant Nicole Dawson. I'm working with Special Agent Quinn. Do you have information for us?"

There was a brief pause. "Yes! I think I have seen the man you are searching for. And the little girl. Only I thought she was a boy."

Nicole sat up straight, her heart hammering in her chest. This could be it! "Ms. Taylor, we're on our way. Where are you?"

The woman hesitated. "Actually, I'm on the road. I had a meeting."

Nicole sighed with disappointment, then Jack interjected, "Every minute counts. What if you answer a few questions now and then meet with us? Are you far from the Sutter Springs Police Department?"

"About fifteen or twenty minutes, I guess. I hadn't thought…"

"It's really important." Jack started the vehicle. "Ms. Taylor, every minute counts," he repeated. "A child is missing."

After hemming and hawing, the woman agreed. They peppered her with some preliminary questions and then Jack disconnected the call and looked across the seat at Nicole's face. They were too stunned to speak for a minute.

"Jack, she thinks she saw Leah."

"Let's get to the station."

A few minutes later, he slid into the parking lot of the police station and the two of them raced inside and passed through the main room, heading straight to the chief's office. When they knocked on his door, he bid them to enter immediately.

"Sergeant. Special Agent. What information do you have?"

Nicole felt out of breath as she told him about the phone call with the woman. "She'll be here in a few minutes."

Excitement spread across his face. "Excellent news. Use the small conference room. If she has credible information, use whatever resources you need."

Ten minutes later, Nicole sat across the table from the young woman, waiting for Jack to return from a coffee run. The Keurig machine was gone, and no one had found the time to replace it yet. Therefore, anyone wanting java needed to make a special trip to the Tim Hortons café across the street.

The woman kept sneaking peeks at Nicole, almost as if she were checking to see if she were really seeing straight. Nicole hadn't had time to change, so she was still dressed as an Amish woman.

Whenever one of her colleagues walked by, she was treated to a smirk. It was getting old very fast.

The door opened and Jack entered, juggling three medium coffees with lids. He set them down on the table before claiming the chair next to Nicole.

"Thank you, Jack." She looked at their guest. "Ms. Taylor, why don't you go ahead and tell us what you heard and saw, as best as you can."

Ms. Taylor looked about forty or forty-five. Her hair was short and shaped in a trendy style. By the cut of her pencil skirt, silk blouse and blazer, Nicole guessed she held a professional job. The fact that she'd come in during her lunch hour spoke of her seriousness. In addition, she'd already given enough details over the phone, details the press didn't have yet, to convince Nicole her claim was legitimate.

"I was in the Plain and Simple Bed and Breakfast yesterday. I had a meeting there. They have a conference room they rent out for events." She glanced at Nicole, as if she were waiting for some kind of affirmation.

Nicole bit back a smile. "I see. Please go on."

The woman nodded. "Yes, well, I was meeting several other people when a man came in. He looked like an electrician. I thought I'd seen him before, but couldn't be sure. He was walking around as if he was checking on things. As he did, he stopped a young pregnant woman. Adele, her name was."

Nicole sat up straighter. "Adele King. Yes, I know her."

Adele, who happened to be very pregnant. This was not a good sign.

"Did he ask her any personal questions? Questions about when she was there, who she lived with, anything like that?"

Ms. Taylor blinked. "Why, yes. Now that you mention it. I particularly remember him talking to her about her schedule. She told him that she was at the bed-and-breakfast in the mornings because the regular girl had quit but went home after lunch each day."

Jack had been leaning back in his chair. At this information, he straightened. "Did he say anything after that?"

She frowned, concentrating. "Well, her uncle came in while they were chatting. Adele left and he had asked for confirmation that the man would be staying through tomorrow only."

That was yesterday. He was leaving today. Sweat broke out around Nicole's collar. They had a slim margin.

"You said that you saw Leah."

She smiled. "Yes, Sergeant. This morning as I was leaving, I saw a blue car in the bed-and-breakfast parking lot. There was no one in it I thought, but then I saw the little one in the back seat. She looked very sad."

She was sad, but she was alive and close by.

They thanked Ms. Taylor and left her with another officer to get her statement.

Nicole and Jack ran from the station and hopped in his car. They had to find Adele. The chief had now promised to send Beck their way, as well. Nicole could hardly sit still on the way to the bed-and-breakfast. They were so close.

Dean Burkholder jerked upright in astonishment when they rushed inside the B and B a few minutes later.

"Adele. We need to see Adele," Nicole burst out.

"She left for home a few minutes ago, Sergeant."

When they asked for her address, the man gave them a brief description of how to get there. "She walks every day, so you might catch her on foot."

They thanked him and rushed out again. They were nearly to the car when Jack's phone rang.

He looked at it. "It's Tanner. I'd nearly forgotten he'd be discharged and back at work today."

"Go ahead and take it." She gritted her teeth. "It might be important."

He opened the call and spoke rapidly. "Tanner, make it quick."

She paused in her pacing as his eyes nearly popped out of his head.

"When? Are you sure... They were... Did they see her? What about him?"

The longer he was on the phone, the jumpier she became. It was obvious that whatever was being said, it was urgent. His hands were shaking with excitement.

He turned to her and said, "I'll let her know. This changes everything."

FIFTEEN

Jack hung up his phone, dazed, and faced Nicole. He had to try twice before he could force the words from between his numb lips. If they were wrong, this could be devastating. She shifted from one foot to the other in front of him, almost dancing in her impatience.

"Jack, what is it? What did Tanner have to say?"

"They have a lead on Leah." He took her hands in his, noting how cold they were. His own were shaking. His eyes were stinging. He blinked until her face came back into focus. "Nicole, someone else has spotted Leah."

Her eyes flared wide, and her mouth dropped open. The shudder that whipped through her body and into her hands told him how much his words affected her. "What! Oh! Tell me."

"A post office worker was on her rounds an hour ago and stopped at a gas station. While she was pumping her gas, she looked over and she saw a small child alone in a green car. The child looked familiar. She couldn't get too close because a man wearing a baseball cap and a plaid shirt was nearby. He looked mad, so she hurried into the store and paid. But she saw his car as it pulled away and wrote down the license plate number. When she got back to the post office, she saw the sketches Fran had made and made the connection of where she'd seen the child before. It was Leah, she thinks, but her hair had been cut very short."

"A green car? I thought it was blue."

He nodded. "Either one of them got it wrong, or the transfer has been made. Either way, we have two leads we have to chase now."

His stomach bottomed out. Who should they go after? Adele or Leah?

"Did anyone follow up on the license plate?" Her grip on his hands grew painful. He didn't complain. He'd let her hold on as hard as she needed to. He could handle a little discomfort if it brought her some relief.

"They did. Tanner found them. He's a whiz with the computer. He not only found the license plate, but he found the residence connected with it. Honey, she is less than forty-five minutes from here, but they don't know how long they'll stay in one place."

Nicole's eyes flashed. "Not long. He knows we're after him. He's already killed his accomplice. If we don't move now, we'll miss our opportunity. Maybe forever."

Unfortunately, every instinct he possessed said she was right. "Tanner's too far away. If we—"

She shook her head. "I know we're supposed to stay together, but we have to split up."

The bottom fell out of his stomach. He went cold from the inside out. "Nicole…"

"Jack, what choice do we have? We've already spent too much time standing here talking. Adele is in danger, too. You heard the chief earlier. They're spread thin. And this case, it's ours—we need to bring them in."

He hated this. "You're right."

"I'll go after Adele. Maybe if he's with the baby, then no one will be there when I find her. You go after Leah. I think she's in more danger. And you need your car. Quickly!"

Without thinking about the appropriateness of his actions or worrying about the future, Jack placed his hands on her cheeks, leaned down and kissed her, telling her with his kiss everything he couldn't—wouldn't—put back into words. His heart warmed when he felt her response.

Just for a second, then he pulled away and backed toward his car. "You be careful, Nicole. Please, don't take any risks that aren't one hundred percent necessary."

"Same goes, Jack." She patted her apron. "Don't forget, I have a gun. I can take care of myself. Now go find that little girl."

He whirled away and jumped into his car, then started the ignition. He watched her sprinting through the grass toward the King farm as he left the driveway.

She'd be well. She had to be. And the chief would be sending more help.

He plugged the address into the GPS then punched the button to bring up Tanner's phone. When his buddy answered, he didn't waste any time. "On my way to the last location I received. Any changes?"

"No. I'm on my way there, so is a black-and-white. You'll beat us there by a lot, though."

Jack disconnected and pressed his foot down on the gas pedal. He had to make good time or it was all for nothing. He followed the map on his dashboard, his gut clenching as he drew closer.

He wouldn't let his mind drift back to Nicole. As soon as he got Leah, he'd go back to her and help her, if she still needed it.

A car pulled out on the road ahead of him.

It was the car that Leah had been seen in. The driver didn't seem to be in a hurry. Was it possible that the driver didn't realize they were being followed? They weren't speeding. He frowned. Was Leah still in the car?

As if in answer to his question, a tiny fist waved in the air. She was in the car. He took in a deep breath, his chest expanding with joy and frenzied relief flowing in with the oxygen. She was still there, and she was alive.

He kept behind the car. If he chased the vehicle, a crash might ensue. Leah might be injured or worse. No, his best choice would be to shadow the car and make his move once they were stopped.

His only fear was that there might be weapons fired on the scene. He called in and gave Tanner his location. "I'm going to keep this phone call going, Tanner. Try and meet me. I don't want to go in without backup, but you know I will. I will not lose this baby."

"I hear you. But don't do anything foolish," Tanner said.

A pause. Then Tanner's voice came back sharp over the phone. "What do you mean alone? Where's Nicole?"

Jack sighed. "We got a tip that Adele King, another pregnant Amish woman, was in danger, and that she may have been taken. Nicole is going back to the King farm to check it out. Do you want to send some backup that way?"

"On it."

Jack relaxed. Nicole wouldn't be going in alone. Whoever went to meet her, they'd have their guns and their badges to back her up. Hopefully, she'd find Adele before any harm came to the young Amish woman, get her safely home and meet him back at the station this afternoon.

The car ahead of him veered off the main road. He kept his distance, turning casually behind the car, not speeding up even when the other car went a little faster.

Then the car made a sudden swerve, taking a turn at full speed, and Jack knew he'd been made. He gave up all pretense of being casual and floored it, racing after the car. They bounced around the back roads for five miles. Jack felt every bump as the car jolted and shook, but he couldn't slow down.

The car ahead of him suddenly swung onto a gravel road.

"Slow down! Can't he see that?"

There was a high level of gravel down the center of the road, a sign that the township had recently sent a grader machine here. The fresh gravel hadn't had a chance to spread out evenly, making the surface as slippery as a coating of black ice.

In horror, Jack watched the car spin and twist like a pinball being pinged around inside a game. The driver didn't seem to understand how to compensate and was probably panicking. Finally, the front end dipped into the ditch along the side of the road, leaving the back passenger tire spinning a foot off the ground.

Jack pulled up behind the car and carefully exited, using his car as a barricade that he could hide behind.

The driver door swung open. Jack raised his weapon,

ready to shoot if he needed to. He said a quick prayer that he wouldn't need to fire it. If he did, he'd aim to injure, not kill, the perp. He startled when a young kid fell from the driver's side of the car. He couldn't have been more than eighteen.

"Stop! FBI! Hands up!" Jack shouted.

The teenager took one look at Jack and tried to make a run for it. He didn't get far. Jack caught up with him and had him subdued when Tanner's vehicle showed up. Jack had no problem turning the kid over to his squad mate so he could go fetch Leah.

He had to unlock the back door using the control panel on the driver's side. When he heard the click from the rear of the car, he jumped back to pull the door open. He blinked past the sudden moisture clouding his vision when Leah Hilty gazed at him. Her brown eyes, just like her mama's, were huge and scared in her sweet little face. Her hair had been shorn to only a couple inches in length, but he would have known her anywhere.

"It's okay, honey." He bent forward slowly, trying to be as unthreatening as he could. His heart broke when she pressed herself against the car seat away from him. The poor baby had been traumatized. Her lower lip trembled. "Shhh. I'm going to take you to your mama. Let me just unhook this seat belt, and we can be on our way."

Her big eyes lit up at the word *mama*. "*Mamm*. Me want *Mamm*."

"I know you want your mother. I'm going to see that it happens."

He clicked on the buckle and it came undone with a sharp snap. Reaching into the car, he gently slid his hands under her armpits and lifted her out of the vehicle and held her close. She was trembling. He tucked her head under his chin and rocked her, rubbing her back the way he'd done with Chloe when she had been sad or hurt.

Leah stopped crying after a couple of minutes and snuggled closer. When she went limp, he realized she'd gone to sleep, the ultimate gesture of trust.

He walked toward his squad mate and friend. The teen who'd been driving the car was already secure in Tanner's vehicle.

"Let's get this kiddo checked out and return her to her mama."

"Good idea. Maybe we can have someone get her mother and meet us at the hospital?"

He nodded. "Can you get her car seat? I'll take her in my car."

Five minutes later, Leah was safely tucked into his car and they were on the way back to Sutter Springs. First, he called Tanner, then Jack called Nicole to give her an update. Until he heard her voice, he didn't realize how tense he was.

"You're okay."

She laughed. "You worry too much. I'm fine. What I want to know is, did you find Leah?"

"I did." He grinned when she whooped in his ear. It was about time they had something to celebrate. "She's conked out in my back seat right now. I already talked with Tanner. He's arranging for someone to bring her mom to the hospital to meet us there."

"Hold on a sec." He heard her talking to someone but guessed that she'd covered the microphone with her hand because the words were muffled. She returned a second later.

"I'm with Adele. Our guy had chased her, but she managed to evade him. I'm walking with her back to her father's house now. You can send a car for me there when you're done."

"Tanner had someone coming to get you for backup—"

"No need. We can literally see the house from here. Have the backup go and get Lucy. They've been separated long enough."

She hung up.

He laughed. She was very good at giving orders.

He checked his rearview mirror. Leah was still sound asleep. He hummed under his breath and drove to the Sutter Springs hospital. He pulled under the carport, and two nurses rushed out to meet him.

Leah woke up when the car door opened. The nurse closest to the car reached in for her. She screamed. Jack didn't even stop to consider what he was doing. He reacted, his heart pounding as that shrill shriek of fear reverberated in his brain. Shouldering the nurse aside, he picked the toddler up.

She quieted and stuck her thumb in her mouth.

"Sorry, ladies. I didn't mean to cut in, but she's used to me now."

Laughing, they stepped aside and ushered him into the emergency room. He sat with Leah against his shoulder for half an hour before the ER doctor came in. With a slightly harried manner, the doctor began his examination.

A few minutes into it, a commotion outside the cubicle caught Jack's attention. He glanced up as the curtain was shoved aside and Lucy flew into the small area, Officer Beck three paces behind her.

"Leah!"

"Mamm! Mamm!" The toddler struggled to free herself from the doctor and wiggle off the table. He lifted her up and deposited her into her mother's arms. Lucy smiled at him, though Jack very much doubted she could see anyone through the haze of tears.

He stood and squeezed past them.

"Danke," Lucy said.

"You're welcome, Mrs. Hilty. Officer Beck here will drive you back to your sister's house when you're finished here."

Exhaustion set in. Jack waved at everyone and left the ER. It was time to go to the station and finish this. He realized this might be the last time he saw Nicole before he left. Shoulders drooping, he walked out of the hospital, the joy he'd felt an hour earlier gone.

Nicole wandered out to the back steps, wondering when Adele's family would be home. There'd been no one there when they'd arrived two hours ago, which wasn't unusual. After all, no one in the family had any reason to suspect Adele was in danger. They were all at work still.

Shouldn't an officer be back for her by now?

She sighed, knowing the officers at the police station were stretched thin. It could be a while. She needed to be patient.

She knew why she was anxious. She wanted to see Jack one last time before he left to let him know she held no bitterness toward him. In fact, she knew her mother's experiences had colored her view, unfairly in his case.

Unfortunately, she couldn't change her upbringing. She loved him, but it wouldn't be enough to overcome a lifetime of doubt and suspicion.

She'd have to be satisfied with seeing him one last time before she let him go for good.

She started back into the house, when a noise caught her attention. It was an engine, but not like a car or a truck. This engine was more like a motorcycle. And it wasn't coming from the road. It was coming from the field beside the house.

Someone was heading toward them—someone who shouldn't be there.

Adrenaline kicked into overdrive. Ducking back into the house, Nicole found Adele in the front room. She startled when Nicole ran toward her.

"We have to go. Now."

"Why do we need to leave?" Adele asked, setting aside her needlework and rising to her feet, using the arms of the chair to push herself out of it.

"I'll explain when we're gone. Let's move! No! Not out back. We need to use the front door."

Adele blinked at the bark in her voice but complied. They ran out the door without grabbing anything from the house. Nicole made them press on, trudging through yards rather than taking the road. She felt bad making a pregnant woman move so fast, but right now she was bent on survival.

She wished she could get her service weapon out. However, she needed both hands to help Adele. She worried about how she'd be able to defend them if they were cornered, but she couldn't do anything about it now.

"Someone was coming to your house, Adele. They were coming on a motorcycle, or maybe an ATV. And they were traveling through the fields."

Adele blanched. "And do you think it was the man who took Lucy and her Leah?"

Nicole caught the Amish woman's elbow, guiding her as she stumbled. "I do. I don't mean to scare you, but you're a target. We have to get you to safety, Adele. You aren't safe alone, not while this is still an issue."

By *this* she meant a group of people set on abducting pregnant women to steal and sell their babies. She didn't have the heart to put it that bluntly. Adele understood enough to keep moving, even when her skin grew damp and her breathing labored. Nicole's dress was sticking to her back and tendrils of her thick hair had escaped her braid and were plastered to her neck.

She didn't slow down.

"You're doing great, Adele. Just keep walking." Nicole kept up a steady stream of encouragement. She could not afford to let the woman have a chance to rest. Their pursuer wasn't hampered by being on foot.

A low hum was coming at them from behind.

Urgency sent her pulse racing. "Quick, Adele! Deeper into the trees."

Without complaint, Adele obeyed. They made it to the tree line not a moment too soon. Squatting down, they held their breath as the ATV whisked by, only inches from where they had been walking a few moments before.

Nicole flung her arm behind her, pointing. "What's in that direction?"

Adele stood, resolve stamped on her delicate features. "My cousin Levi lives back in that direction."

Nicole perked up. "Levi Burkholder? I know him. Would he be home?"

"*Jah*, he would. Levi is a deacon in the church now. He has a meeting in his home weekly around this time."

"Sounds promising."

"First we'll have to pass through Ivan Schrock's farm."

"Will he mind?"

"*Nee*. Ivan is a *gut* man. He would never turn us away."

Exactly what she wanted to hear. "Then that is where we are going."

They started back through the trees. The tall sugar maples blotted out the sun. They found a shallow path, most likely plodded out by deer and other animal traffic. Roots and branches scattered around them and became a constant tripping hazard.

Still, they trudged on. Unaccustomed to the boots she had been given for this assignment, Nicole felt her feet beginning to ache. She was getting hungry, too. Both sensations she ignored.

They cleared the trees and entered Ivan Schrock's farm. A dog barked wildly beyond the house. Glancing around, she saw a buggy, but no movement.

"Is he home, do you think?"

Adele panted, her hand on her stomach. "*Jah*. He's home. I thought he would *cumme* and greet us."

Hearing the roar of an ATV again, the two women hurried deeper into the property, determined to reach Levi Burkholder's place. For a moment, they flattened themselves against the back of the barn, barely daring to breathe as the jarring hum of the ATV ventured closer before finally drifting away from them.

When it was finally gone and Nicole deemed it safe to continue, they moved slowly away from the barn and traveled closer to Adele's cousin's house.

Adele suddenly tripped. Nicole caught her and kept her upright. She looked down.

When Adele opened her mouth to scream, Nicole placed a hand over her mouth to keep the sound trapped inside. They'd found Ivan Schrock. It was unclear at first what had killed him, but Nicole didn't doubt he was murdered. His face was a mask of fear.

The ATV was coming back.

"You have to continue to your cousin's house," Nicole whispered in Adele's ear. "Does your cousin have a community phone nearby?"

Adele nodded, tears streaming down her pale cheeks.

"Good. Have your cousin call your father's bed-and-breakfast, then call 911. I'm going to try and call my friend to come and get me."

Right now, she wanted to give Adele enough time to get away. As she looked around, the idea that Brandon had been using Ivan's place as his headquarters settled in. She didn't have proof, but she knew she was right. The way he continually circled back to them felt like a game. He knew they were here. He was playing with them, enjoying their fear.

She wouldn't let him have Adele or her baby.

"What will you do?" Adele held on to her hand.

"Don't worry about me. I need you to get to your family. I can handle things on this end if I know you're safe."

Adele looked like she wanted to argue.

"There's no time to discuss this, Adele. Go! Please. And don't forget to call the police station. I need to know that you made it safely home."

Adele nodded. She helped the expectant mother over a fence, then walked back near the barn.

She needed to call Jack. When she dialed his number, it went to voice mail. Impatient, she listened to his voice telling her to leave a message while keeping one ear listening for the ATV's return.

The message ended and she heard a beep. "Jack. Listen, Adele is safe. But I'm at Ivan Schrock's house. He's dead. And I think the man who killed him is here on the property. I need backup. I need—"

A footstep behind her made her jump and drop the phone. Whirling, she came face-to-face with the man from the sketch. Gazing into his cold eyes, she knew she'd seen him somewhere before. But where?

Her heart was ready to burst through her chest it was beating so fast. Quick as a snake, the man slapped the phone from her hand, then pulled out a gun and shot the device which was now on the ground.

"You'll be making no more calls."

Her gun was in her apron pocket. She needed to figure out how to reach it without him shooting her. She'd have to keep her wits about her.

"You don't even recognize me, do you?" He shook his head. "All this time, I've been concerned about it. I was sure you'd seen me that day. The way you watched that window, I thought you'd recognized me. I had to move around and find a new place. I tried to get rid of you and that Amish lady, but you made it hard. Even grazed my arm, but you must be a bad aim."

She noticed a bulky lump under his sleeve, probably a bandage.

"No worries," he went on. "Your number's up now. Then I'll take care of her."

Suddenly, she knew where she'd seen him. "Brandon Nichols!"

He smiled. It was a very nasty grin. Her blood curdled in her veins. "Bingo. Not that it will do you any good."

He grabbed the shovel standing next to the barn and hoisted it up. She tried to duck out of the way. He brought it down.

Blinding pain filled her head. She collapsed.

SIXTEEN

Nicole had trouble opening her eyes. Her stomach was pressed down against something hard and she felt as if she were on a boat. She always had motion sickness on boats. She would know the sensation, even with her eyes closed. Once had been enough to cement it in her mind.

Why was she on a watercraft?

Her head was pounding like someone had hit it with a sledgehammer, and her shoulders ached. Nicole tried to move her arms and couldn't. That's when she realized she wasn't on a boat. She was being carried. Forcing her burning lids to open, she found herself staring at a wall of baby blue. She was looking at a man's back.

She was upside down, slung over a muscular shoulder. Hard hands held her in place, keeping her from sliding in any direction. Her arms were handcuffed behind her back. The memory flooded back. Brandon Nichols had been the kidnapper and had ambushed her. No wonder he'd looked so familiar to her. They'd gone to college together, years ago. She had not seen him in a long time.

Her memories of him were blurry. They had never been friends, only casual acquaintances who were in several classes together. Did he remember her, too?

Instinct told her he did, that this was no coincidence. This was probably why he'd targeted her, some long-simmering resentment about the past combined with his current need to silence whoever got in his way.

Now that she'd seen him, she knew that the abductor and the man who had been in the police station, working on the electricity were one and the same.

Which meant he'd had plenty of opportunity to try to poison them. It gave her chills thinking how easily he had tampered with coffee the entire police department would drink. She hadn't recognized him from the picture of his planting the car bomb, and he had disguised himself in the office. But seeing him up close like she was now, she connected the threads she'd missed before.

But how was he connected to the black market group?

He was going to kill her! She squirmed to break his hold.

"No use wiggling." Brandon's calm voice floated down from above. "I don't plan on letting you slip away from me. You've ruined everything, you know. My father is very displeased. I promised I'd get rid of you. Then when you are no longer in the picture, I can take care of Lucy."

His father. His father must have been the boss, the man calling the shots and ordering pregnant women be abducted and later murdered.

The casual way Brandon talked about murdering both her and Lucy was chilling. "Lucy didn't do anything to you."

He chuckled.

She shuddered.

"She saw me. She can identify me, and that could put me in prison, which I don't plan on letting her do."

She tried to move again. The only thing that budged was the prayer *kapp* that she'd been wearing. The white piece of material dropped from her head and landed on the ground in the dirt. Frustrated tears stung her eyes. She blinked them away. She didn't have time to waste on emotion. She would probably break down later. If she survived this.

Stop. Think. She had to be smart, find a way out of this mess.

He walked inside a barn and dumped her on the ground like a sack of wheat. She groaned as she landed on her arm. She hadn't been able to use her hands to catch herself like she normally would.

"Sorry." He didn't sound sorry. And the smile he sent her was cold and deadly. "I managed to snag a pair of handcuffs to bind you with when I visited the station. Someone was careless enough to leave them sitting on a desk."

Appeal to our past acquaintance. "Brandon, why are you doing this? We know each other. Went to school together."

It didn't work. "Hmm. Yes, we did. Unfortunately, you were too wrapped up in your ambition to pay any attention to me. I'll bet you wished you had now, huh? Not only am I getting wealthy, while you are stuck in a dead-end job, but I also hold the power of life and death over you." He softened his voice. "I never wanted this for you, Nicky. But you brought it on yourself."

She recalled he planned to go after Lucy again.

The acid in her gut churned. "Look, you don't have to worry about Lucy. Lucy is Amish. She wouldn't testify against you."

He hunkered down next to her, so close his breath

fanned her face. "Do you really think I'm going to risk it? Besides, when my father says get rid of all loose ends, he means it." He frowned. "She and her baby are being protected by the police now. That's too bad. It wouldn't have helped my case if I could have presented my father with a newborn." His gaze hardened. "You have stolen two from me now. That woman from the bed-and-breakfast would have been perfect."

He was talking about Adele.

Relief coursed through her at his unwitting confirmation that the young Amish woman had gotten back to her family safely. She knew the Burkholder family, and Adele's husband would protect her and her unborn child. Even if she didn't escape herself, at least the civilians she had been intent on protecting had made it out.

She hadn't failed.

Brandon stood. His patience was up. "Don't go away."

He left the room. She heard metal scraping and an engine hum. Nicole did her best to move. Twice, she almost rose to her knees, but her head injury made her dizzy and she couldn't keep her balance. She slumped back down to the ground.

A chuckle announced his return.

"Poor Nicky." She hated the name Nicky, but it was the least of her worries. "You really think you can get away from me? Sorry, sweetheart. I have plans for you. Unfortunately, it won't be pleasant. You've caused me too much trouble to be shown mercy. Okay, it's been fun chatting with you, but I have plans today," he repeated. "Which means your time is up."

She tried to scoot back away from him, but it was no use. He was stronger, faster and unhampered by handcuffs or a head injury. She wasn't going to go to her death compliantly. When he loomed over her, she kicked out with her legs. He grunted when one boot found purchase. Other than that, he didn't seem to notice her efforts. He grabbed her upper arms and yanked her to her feet.

"Brandon, please!"

He ignored her pleas. His face lost all expression and his eyes went flat, reminding her of a timber rattlesnake preparing to strike its victim.

Struggling, she tried to break his hold. It was no use. He dragged her from the barn and into a large round metal structure. She thought it was a silo at first, but it was too short. He pushed her to the center of the room. She stepped onto what looked like a patch of grain.

And stumbled into a hole. She was up to her knees in grain!

Brandon turned and left her there, shutting the door and locking her in.

She'd never been in a grain bin or silo before, although she'd heard of people suffocating in grain. Still, it wasn't deep. If she could climb out, she should be okay. Maybe buy herself enough time for Jack to get her message and come after her.

It was difficult to get her feet and legs to do what she wanted. The grain was thick and heavy, and she didn't have her arms to help her maneuver.

Something hummed. Glancing around the room, her mouth went dry and her heart thudded in her chest. Her hands were slick as she fought to pull them from the constraining handcuffs. It was no use.

He didn't intend to starve her. He planned to bury her.

A thin stream of grain poured down from a narrow

conveyor belt several feet above her head. Fear kicked into overdrive. It was a slim thread falling, but she'd watched water fill up a sink enough times to know it wouldn't take long before the grain rose high enough to fill the entire area.

She'd never be able to escape on her own. Not with the handcuffs on.

Desperate, she began to scream for help.

Brandon hadn't shot her; he wanted her to suffer. Maybe someone would come by and hear her screaming. Tears dripped down her cheeks, but she couldn't do anything about them. Her headache worsened with each yell, but she couldn't stop.

She had no idea how much time she had left.

Jack and Tanner were working combing through the leads they had collected over the past two days. They were close to finding the second kidnapper. He could feel it in his bones. Reuniting Leah with her mother had been a shot in the arm he'd needed to get reinvigorated. He couldn't wait to tell Nicole the story when she returned.

They halted what they were doing when they heard the chief yelling from his office. Jack lifted his head as the chief burst into the room where his officers were working.

All activity stopped and everyone focused on Chief Spencer.

"Drop everything!" he bellowed. "Adele King is safe and with her family."

The immediate cheer was cut short when he gestured wildly for them to stop. "I just got a call from her husband's business. Sergeant Dawson found her and helped her escape. However, the sergeant didn't get out. She's still in danger. At the Schrock farm. Adele said they found the body of Mr. Schrock."

Jack reached for his phone to text Nicole. It wasn't there! He'd left it charging in his car!

Heart thudding, Jack raced out of the police station, barely aware of Tanner hard on his heels.

Yanking the key fob out of his pocket, he pressed the unlock button several times in quick succession as he approached his Escape. In his SUV, he made quick work of grabbing his phone and checking his messages. One from Nicole. Praying as he leaned against the door, he tapped in his passcode with shaking fingers and listened to it. When her voice cut off, he swayed.

Nicole was in danger, possibly alone with a killer. He had to get out of here.

Nicole. She needed him. He could hear her voice again, telling him she was at the farm and that she'd found a body and that she was being followed.

He was inside the car with no memory of opening the door. Tanner jumped into the passenger side.

Jack began backing up before Tanner's door was closed completely. Yelping, the other special agent shut his door and buckled himself in. As they spun out of the parking lot, the station doors swung open and other officers swarmed into the lot, heading for their cars.

The whole department was coming out to save her.

"Where are we going?" Tanner demanded.

"Nicole is trapped at the Schrock farm, and she thinks she found the body of Ivan Schrock. She called to tell me she got Adele out, but her message cut off. But before it did, she said she was certain someone is there with her. She's in danger, Tanner. Someone is trying to kill her. Pretty sure it's Brandon."

He'd failed her.

"We'll get there, buddy." Tanner kept trying to calm him down. "Let's be rational about this. We can't just tear off anytime we want."

Jack wasn't in the mood to listen. "You don't know that she'll be fine or that we'll get there in time. We might already be too late. Why would she go there alone? Why didn't I check my messages earlier?"

He gagged, his mind twisting away from the images of Nicole dead. He couldn't think that way. If he did, he'd be no good to her or anyone else. He needed clarity.

He pounded the heel of his hand against the steering wheel as anguish swirled inside him.

He'd gone back to the station and had conferred with the chief and with Tanner. Looking back, it seemed to him he'd chatted with nearly the entire department before he'd realized Nicole needed him.

He took a curve at sixty miles an hour. Beside him Tanner yelled in alarm.

"Jack, slow down!"

"She's in the path of a murderer, Tanner. I can't slow down. I can't take it easy. All I can do is get there as soon as I can to do my best and keep the woman I love alive."

The car was silent except for the thrumming sound of rocks and gravel churning under the tires, sometimes kicking up and hitting the underside of the SUV.

Finally, Tanner broke the silence. "I'm sorry, Jack. I didn't understand how it was for you."

Jack sighed. "We were engaged once. Before Beverly died."

"Do you think—"

He shook his head. "I will love her for as long as I live, but we have no hope. Not while I have a career where I have to keep secrets. She doesn't trust me, and I can't force her to. I will have to be happy knowing she is well in the world. I think we can be friends, though."

Except it wouldn't be enough for him.

God, I will accept being just friends with her. All I ask is please let her be all right. Let her live, Lord.

It was a cry from his very soul. Tanner kept up a steady stream of calm monologue. Every few comments, Jack grunted in response. He wasn't truly listening. His attention was securely focused on getting to Nicole.

She was strong. Competent. A brilliant strategist. All of which would help her in any battle she became involved in.

She also had a heart the size of Texas and would willingly risk her life five times over if she could save an innocent.

That was the cost of being in law enforcement. A cost he knew well, and believed in. He'd step in front of a bullet for Nicole.

Beside him, Tanner was on the radio, calling in their current location and where they were heading. The other units were also en route. Good. He had no idea how much help they'd need, but it was all welcome.

The sense of urgency coursing through his blood became unbearable. Jack pushed his foot down on the pedal and his Escape surged ahead on the back road, dust billowing behind them like a cape. He was functioning on instinct.

When they arrived at the farm, Tanner stumbled

from the car, his face pale and shiny, the collar of his shirt wet with sweat. To his credit, he didn't complain. They spread out, calling for Nicole. Jack was aware of two cruisers pulling in and parking near him, but he didn't cease searching.

"Jack!"

He ran to Tanner. The man was holding a white *kapp* in his hands. "Is this the one she was wearing?"

Jack shrugged, his stomach clenched in a knot. "I don't know. It could be. All the Amish women in the area wear *kapps* like that one."

The cops fanned out.

"What's that humming?" Hansen asked.

Jack tilted his head and listened. It was coming from the left, near the barn. When they approached, they could see the grain bin was being filled.

Jack stopped. Something else was happening. "Listen!"

After a second, they all seemed to hear it. Nicole was screaming for help. Inside the grain bin. Horrified, they ran in that direction. Tanner found the switch and turned off the belt. The hum died out. Nicole shouted louder.

Jack tried the door, but it wouldn't open. Moving quickly, he swung onto the ladder and climbed to the top. Opening the hatch, he looked down. His blood froze in his veins. Nicole's face, pale and exhausted, peered up at him. Her head was tilted back, the grain grazing the underside of her chin. If she lowered her chin, she'd be swallowing the grain.

"Call the fire department!" Jack shouted to the officers below. "We need an auger and a grain rescue tube."

The panels on the tube would keep the grain from

falling in on Nicole so they could remove the grain pressing in on her and free Nicole.

Tanner gave him a thumbs-up.

Jack looked at Nicole. "Okay, honey. We have help coming. Can you lift your arms?"

"Jack." Her voice was hoarse. She looked like she was ten seconds away from passing out. "He handcuffed my hands. Hit me in the head."

For the first time, he noticed the dried blood on her temple. Her chin trembled with the effort to hold it above the grain.

Her eyes blinked slowly. She was going to pass out. If she did, she'd drown in the grain. He remembered thinking he'd take a bullet for her. This would work, too.

"I'm going in. She can't keep her head above the grain level."

Before anyone could stop him, he swung up on the side of the bin and lowered himself in to stand right in front of her. The grain came to his shoulders. His arms weren't stuck in it, so he hooked them around her and took her weight onto himself, allowing her head to rest at a normal level.

They couldn't stay that way for too long, but he'd hold her until help arrived. "Hold on, honey. They're coming to get us."

It seemed to take forever, but help did arrive. A grain rescue tube was set up around them, placed in one side at a time, to keep the grain from collapsing in on them as they were lifted out. It was awkward, but Nicole was lifted first, her handcuffs cut off before she was placed on an ambulance stretcher. By the time Jack was lifted out, she was already in the ambulance.

"Look what we have!"

Jack gazed back and saw the man from Francesca's picture alive and in person, with Officer Beck at his side.

Jack ran and stopped the ambulance from driving away. He had the paramedics open the door and beckoned for Officer Beck to bring the man over. "Nicole? Do you recognize this guy?"

She peeled her lids open. "That's him. Brandon Nichols," she whispered. "His dad runs the operation. I remember him from college. His dad's name is Jeremy Nichols."

"I know you wanted to read him his rights…"

"Let Beck do it. He gets the arrest."

Ahh. Of course. After dealing with Ted's death, Officer Beck was the perfect choice. It was justice. She kept her eyes open until Brandon was led away. Then they fell shut with a sigh. Jack stood back from the ambulance as the door was closed.

"His father was the leader of this operation? Is that what she said?" Jack never took his gaze from the ambulance. When it was out of sight, he turned back to Tanner.

"Yes. Brandon Hatnells—"

"Nichols," Tanner repeated, stunned. "She said his dad's name was Jeremy Nichols. Surely, you've heard of him?"

Jack nodded. "I seem to remember him being some hotshot philanthropist. Never knew he had a son, though."

"You remember correctly," the chief said, coming to stand next to him. "He's well-known and respected in these parts. Which doesn't mean I won't take him and his son down if they're breaking the law."

"You'll get a warrant?"

The chief made the call. Given the circumstances, it didn't take long for the judge to issue one. Two hours later, the Nichols's home and properties were being searched for evidence of criminal activity.

Mrs. Nichols complained and threatened to sue. Until the first body was found, buried in the wishing well that had once been the main source of water for the house but had been filled in years before. There were three bodies total. Two were women who'd been dead for a while, victims of Mr. Nichols's avarice. The third victim shocked them all.

Mrs. Nichols choked back a sob as she recognized her own brother.

It took a while to sort it all out. Jack was whupped by the time he made it to the hospital to talk with Nicole.

"Hi." Her wan smile greeted him.

"Hey." He sauntered over to the bed, his gaze scouring her face.

"Did you get him?" she asked quietly. "Did you get Brandon's father?"

He had expected her to ask right off the bat.

"We got him. We got them all. We had enough evidence of his activities to send him away for a long time. He'd actually buried bodies on his property. Even his brother-in-law. Our guess is the man had seen or heard too much."

"Brandon?"

"At this moment, he has multiple counts of murder, attempted murder, assault and kidnapping against him.

Enough to nail him to the wall. He won't get away with what he did."

She sighed. "You did it. You can go home now and deal with your sister's trial. I hope they put her killer away for a long time." She hesitated. "Where does that leave us?"

"Us?"

She stared at him. "Yes. Us."

His heart stopped. "Nicole, you know I love you. I never stopped. But I have to deal with my sister's murder trial. And I haven't changed jobs. What happens if I have to keep secrets again?"

"I don't know, Jack." Those deep brown eyes glistened. "Maybe we'll figure something out."

It's what she didn't say that ripped him apart.

"You don't trust me."

"It's not—"

"It is." He backed up toward the door. "Nicole, I love you. I know you need time to heal now. I'm not sure what it will take to convince you to trust me, but we can't have a relationship without trust. That's my line in the sand."

Her lips quivered as she stared at him. He stepped forward, kissed her slowly, a kiss he'd always remember, then turned and walked out the door.

He left, stalking out of the hospital, and got into his car. Could he find a way to make her trust him? He wasn't sure it was possible.

He thumped his head back against the headrest. He needed to get through the trial first. Then maybe he'd be able to find his way out of this mess he'd made of his relationship with Nicole.

SEVENTEEN

Three months after he'd left Nicole in Sutter Springs, Jack walked out of the courtroom. It was finished. After almost three years of waiting, the man who'd killed his sister was on his way to prison, and if all worked out the way it should, he would never be free again.

He should have been content with that. His sister's killer was put away, but he doubted he'd ever know who'd hired him. The company that had supplied him with the means to kill Beverly by overlooking his activities had paid Jack a settlement, enough money to make him a rich man.

If he cared for money.

He didn't. All he wanted was to raise his niece in a loving home. And Nicole.

Why had he pushed her away? He'd never find another woman like her. And even if he did, it wouldn't matter. His heart belonged to her, now and forever. There was a constant ache, an emptiness in his life, that only she could fill.

He'd been stubborn and foolish to believe he could forget her. She was in his mind every day—had been since the day he'd walked out of her life years ago. He needed her to be happy.

But that would never happen until he resolved a few issues.

It was Friday afternoon. He'd taken the rest of the day off, but the idea of waiting until Monday and letting his thoughts fester all weekend didn't appeal to him. He'd rather deal with it now, if it was possible.

He approached his car and put his hand on the door handle, waiting for the beep telling him it was now unlocked. After getting in, he turned the engine on and waited for his phone to connect. When it did, he pressed the speed dial number for SAC Mitchell.

On the third ring, she picked up. "Jack. What can I do for you? Everything go all right with the trial?"

He cleared his throat. "Yes, ma'am. I'm back in my car, ready to head out. The trial went well. I was wondering if you'd be available this afternoon? I have something I need to talk with you about. Something that's very important to me."

A lengthy pause followed his statement.

"Yes." She drew the word out. "I can fit you in around two. I'll have an hour free. Will that be enough time?"

"More than enough. Thanks."

"You're not quitting on me, are you, Jack?"

"Not at the moment."

"Meaning you might in the future?" There was no judgment in her voice.

"I have no idea, ma'am. But I'll see you at two." He hung up the phone, relieved and nervous at the same time. He'd started on this path. Now he'd follow it through. He couldn't think of any other way to possibly invite Nicole back into his life.

And even then, he didn't know if she'd accept. Not after what he'd put her through, for the second time.

He winced. The only way to find out was to keep going. A quick glance at his dashboard told him he had enough time to swing by his apartment and check in on Chloe before his appointment with the SAC.

When he walked in the door, Chloe glanced up from her spot on the floor where she'd been watching her favorite cartoon. A bright grin lit her face like the sun.

"Uncle Jack!" Scrambling to her feet, the little girl threw herself at her uncle's legs for a hug. He didn't disappoint, picking her up and lifting her high above his head before catching her close. She giggled.

"Jack, we didn't expect you here this early." Joyce stood in the kitchen doorway, drying her hands on a dishrag, her reading glasses perched on her head.

"I didn't plan it, but it worked out." He set Chloe down. "Hey, sweetie, I need to talk with Joyce for a few minutes. Okay?"

She skipped back to her cartoon. Jack waited until she was settled and followed Joyce into the kitchen.

"The trial?"

"All good. He's going to prison for the rest of his life."

"Good." She nodded, then narrowed her eyes. "But that's not why you're here."

She knew him well. "No. I was wondering if you could watch Chloe longer than usual for me? Possibly overnight?"

He'd had her watch Chloe overnight while he'd been

in Sutter Springs three months before, but that was work related. This was personal.

"Of course. You know I can. Any special reason why?"

He smiled tightly, holding his emotions in check. "If things go well, when I return, I will be on my way to getting engaged again."

Joyce's hands flew to her mouth. "Nicole?"

He'd talked about his former fiancée more than he'd thought. "Yeah. But I have to work some things out first. A prayer or two wouldn't hurt."

"You got it. You've been alone too long, Jack Quinn. It's time you settled down and gave that little girl in there a family."

"My thoughts exactly."

He packed a change of clothes and his toiletries, then hugged Chloe. "Be good and listen to Joyce."

"I will, Uncle Jack."

Having kissed his niece's soft cheek, he left, striding purposefully to his car to make the trip into work. His heart was hammering in his chest the entire journey from the parking garage to Delores Mitchell's office. It was a good thing he hadn't worn a tie today. Having that constrictive piece of material around his throat would have choked him.

"Hi, Marci." He approached the receptionist's desk. "I have an appointment with SAC Mitchell at two."

She smiled up at him, a kind-faced woman in her early fifties. She had a picture of her husband and son on her desk, but no other personal effects. "She's on the phone at the moment, Jack. But as soon as she's done, you can go in."

He had to wait for less than two minutes. Just enough

time to calm his inner anxiety before he was ushered into his superior's office. She gestured to the chair in front of her desk, and he sat, waiting for her to begin.

"So, Jack." She set her glasses on the desk and leaned back in her chair. "You have me curious. What's on your mind that couldn't wait until Monday?"

Jack shifted in his seat and cleared his throat. Now that he was here, sitting before her, he was unsure where to begin. "Well, first of all, the trial went well. Thanks for being so understanding."

It was a ridiculous comment, and he knew it. There was never any doubt that she'd let him have time off. It was a way to start the conversation, though.

And he was hedging, because if she said no, his hopes would all crash and burn around him.

She shrugged. "We're a team. This was important. Enough stalling. What's really on your mind?"

"My ex-fiancée, Nicole Dawson."

Her eyes widened. "Ex-fiancée? The Sergeant Dawson I sent you to work with?"

His lips tightened around a stiff smile. "The same. I apologize that I never told you about her, but it was not a subject I could easily talk about."

"Obviously. Are you getting back together?"

He hesitated. This was where things got dicey. "I think there's a possibility, but there's an issue with my job."

She didn't like that. He could see it in the frown she leveled at him. "What's the problem?"

"You weren't here when I first began. I was undercover, and as part of my cover, I was seen going around with a very attractive woman. She was part of the case

I was working on, one of the people I put into prison, in fact."

"I read about that. Excellent work, breaking up that terrorist cell."

"Thank you." He rubbed his hand through his hair. "It was classified work, and my previous supervisor told me under no circumstances could I discuss the case with anyone, including Nicole, despite our relationship and her occupation. Nicole saw the pictures. Some of them were pretty bad. And I couldn't deny that I'd cheated on her without revealing classified information. She broke our engagement. I don't think I can ever go back to her if I can't be completely honest with her about what happened."

Compassion shone from Mitchell's face. "That stinks, Jack."

He nodded, his stomach already sinking. Was he doomed to fail?

But she wasn't done. "Look, that case was several years ago. The woman you were with is in prison, as is her entire family. I'll clear it, but I think I can release you from that burden, but only with Nicole. We don't want to advertise that you're a special agent. You know what I mean?"

"I know." He had to speak around the sudden lump in his throat as hope grew in his chest. He hadn't lost his opportunity to win his love back.

"Okay, give me some time to make a call or two."

Some of his excitement morphed into impatience. How much time was "some"?

"Do you need me to go home and wait?" He could hear the strain in his voice.

"No. Wait in the reception area. If I can get you the answers today, I will."

He nodded his thanks and returned to prowl around the reception area under Marci's amused gaze. He was too keyed up to sit in the plush chairs. He waited for nearly twenty minutes before SAC Mitchell called him back into her office.

She greeted him with a satisfied grin. "Well, Special Agent Quinn. It looks like you're making a trip to Sutter Springs." She raised her eyebrows. "I expect to be invited to the wedding."

Nicole kicked her apartment door closed behind her, then winced. Her neighbors weren't going to be pleased with her. She carried the plastic bags filled with groceries to the kitchen counter and began putting them away. Rain splattered against her window, matching her mood perfectly.

Actually, she'd been in a funk for three months now, ever since she let Jack walk away again. Time after time, she'd started to call him, to tell him that she believed him and knew he hadn't cheated on her. She trusted him.

The only thing that had held her back was guilt. Guilt that she had let her insecurities prevent her from recognizing what a fine man he was. He had too much integrity to do what she'd accused him of. And who better than a cop to know about classified work? He was in the FBI. There were bound to be things he couldn't tell anyone, not even a fiancée, or a spouse.

Her mood darkened with the word. Thunder rumbled overhead.

She should have been the one person he felt safe with, regardless of what missions his job sent him on.

She'd failed him in a spectacular way. How did one ask for forgiveness and a second chance?

Fear held her back. Now that she had realized her error, she didn't know how to reach out to him, nor if he would even want her to. What if she'd killed the love he had for her? He'd told her he loved her, and she'd turned her back on him.

Hot tears filled her eyes. She blinked them back. Once she put the remaining groceries away, she turned off the kitchen light and walked to the living room. Brushing aside the curtains, she stared out, past the rain splashing the window and running down like tears. It was almost seven, although the weather made it seem much later due to the darkness. On a bright day, the sun wouldn't set until around eight in August.

She sighed.

Her phone was burning a hole in her pocket. Pulling it out, she stared at it like it was a living creature capable of biting her. Should she? If she called him, at least she'd know if he'd listen to her apology and maybe if he still had any affection for her.

Biting her lip, she fought with herself for five full minutes before finally giving in and dialing. She knew the number by heart.

She hit Call and almost panicked and hung up when it rang. Before she could, he answered.

"Nicole?" His voice was a bit choked, as if he were struggling with some strong emotion.

She hesitated.

"Nicole? Please, honey, I need to hear your voice. Are you all right?"

The breath she'd been holding left her in a whoosh. All at once, the tears she'd been holding back spilled over her bottom lashes and streamed down her cheeks. "Jack."

"I'm here."

She sniffed. "I'm a fool."

A startled laugh left him. How she wished she could see his face! "Never that, Nicole."

Leaning her forehead against the cool window, she closed her eyes. "I let my own fears and lack of confidence play with my mind. Jack, I know that you were telling me the truth. I know that you didn't betray me. I was just so confused. I don't know what I was thinking."

His sigh reverberated down the line. "It means a lot to hear that. You have no idea how much."

She sagged a little, relieved he didn't sound angry or upset. Really, he sounded happy.

"Where do we go from here?"

Please don't reject me now.

A warm chuckle came through the phone. "Well, for starters, you could open your front door."

"What?"

He hung up. She took the phone away from her ear and frowned for a second. Someone knocked on her door, three staccato raps. Her heart bumped. She crossed the room and opened the door and came face-to-face with Jack's beloved grin.

"Jack. What are you doing here?" Joy shot through her.

"What? Aren't you happy to see me?"

She rolled her eyes. "You know I am. I never expected to see you again, though. Not after how awful I was to you."

He smiled and ran a finger down her cheek. "You going to invite me in?"

She stepped aside and let him enter. His face was thinner. He'd lost weight in the past three months. But then, so had she.

He turned back to her. "To answer your question, I'm here because I couldn't stay away. At the same time, I didn't think I could return to you until I was able to be completely honest."

Nicole rushed forward and placed her fingers on his lips. "But I don't need you to now. I know you have things you can't tell me. I will never again ask you to reveal those. It was selfish of me. I know you have classified information you can't tell anyone."

He kissed the fingers touching his mouth. She shivered.

"I appreciate it, and I am sure there will be more things like it in the future. However, I can share what happened with that particular case. I got permission from the higher-ups to tell you."

She widened her eyes, shocked he'd go through that for her. "I wouldn't have asked you to do that."

Then she grimaced. She hadn't given him much choice, though.

"You have a right to know, and since the case is done, I've been cleared to tell you. I came as soon as I got word. I'm staying at the hotel in town, so I have plenty of time to answer any questions you may have. But it goes no further."

"Absolutely." She was still slightly off-kilter because he was here.

Reaching out, he took her hand and tugged, leading her to sit with him on the couch. He dropped her hand when he arranged himself on the middle cushion, stretching his long legs out in front of himself.

The urge to grab his hand back rocketed through her, but she resisted. She settled herself against the corner, angling her body so she could watch him, still unable to believe he was here again, sitting inches away from her.

He began to speak. "I was still working at the police department when I was approached by the FBI to work with them to catch this small cell dipping into terrorism. They were small potatoes, so to speak, but there was enough money there for them to be a national security threat. I agreed. I mean, why wouldn't I?"

She nodded. Terrorism was a scary thing. To be able to fight against it was not an opportunity to turn down.

"I get it."

"Anyway, I was already too involved to pull out when I was given the order to shadow that woman, see what I could find. I'd been ordered not to say a word."

"And then I started giving you ultimatums." She frowned.

"I wanted to tell you, Nicole. If there was any way, I would have."

She nodded. "You told me enough three months ago that it should have been enough."

He shrugged. "Maybe. I don't know. All I know is that I am finally free to tell you about that. And, to make it even sweeter, Fred Johnson, Beverly's murderer, is behind bars now."

She moved forward then and hugged him. "Oh, Jack. I'm so happy for you. I know you worried he'd get off. But justice has been served."

His somber gaze met hers. "Yes, but it still won't

bring Beverly back. I'll always regret how her life ended."

"Yes, but it wasn't your fault. You know that, right?"

"I do now." He scooched closer to her. "One thing I don't intend to regret is missing another chance to make things right with you. I still love you, Nicole. I never stopped."

Her blood pounded in her ears and her breath caught in her throat. "I never stopped loving you, either, Jack, although I was too angry at first to admit it."

His hand brushed her cheek and lingered on her jaw. "Do you think we can start over, give us another shot?"

"I want to."

He reached back and pulled a solitaire ring out of his pocket. She recognized the band she'd thrown at him when she'd ended their engagement. "Enough to put this back on your finger again?"

She bit her lip to keep a grin in check. "Oh? Why would I do that?"

He rolled his eyes and slid off the couch and onto one knee. "I should have known you'd want the whole thing again. Nicole Dawson, I love you and will for the rest of my life. Marry me?"

She held out her trembling hand, nodding. "Yes, Jack. I would be honored to marry you, and I will never again doubt your integrity."

He slid the ring on her finger. She could hardly breathe around the bubbles of happiness bursting inside her chest.

Jack stood and took her hands. He pulled her to her feet and into his strong arms. "I love you and will never give you a reason to doubt me. I will never betray you or the children we will have together."

She closed her eyes as his head dipped, sighing when his lips brushed hers. She'd marry him as soon as she could so they could start their life together. They'd waited long enough.

When he deepened the kiss, she stopped thinking. They'd work it out.

Later.

EPILOGUE

One year later

"Where are we going?" Nicole reached across the seat to her husband and gently poked him with her finger. She loved the freedom of touching him whenever she wanted to. "We've been driving for over an hour now."

Jack let out a soft laugh. He captured the hand tickling him and raised it to his lips, kissing her knuckles. "I never knew how impatient you were. We're almost there."

He released her hand.

She huffed and fell back against the seat, crossing her arms. She couldn't quite suppress the smile tugging at her lips, which of course ruined her act. Giving up, she laughed.

She was too happy to pretend to be anything else. It was hard to believe they'd been married almost six months. She'd wasted so much time dwelling on the sad fate of her parents' marriage.

"I'll be good. But I have no idea what your big surprise is."

He tossed her a grin that took her breath away. "It'll be worth it. I promise."

"Are we almost there, Uncle Jack?" Chloe whined from the back seat. The six-year-old girl didn't whine often, but when she did, she did it with style.

Nicole bit her lip so she wouldn't smile.

"Soon, Bug. Soon." Jack winked at Nicole. He was as amused by the child as she was.

Nicole turned to look at the niece she'd inherited when she and Jack had married. Chloe had been a solemn child, and no wonder. She'd blossomed, though, since they'd become a family. Her nightmares had dwindled in frequency. Once a month, Nicole and Jack accompanied her to a counselor. The counselor was pleased with the little girl's progress and had started suggesting they wean her off the sessions.

At first, Nicole had been terrified to take on the duties of a mother figure to the traumatized child. But Chloe was a joy from the first day. She didn't seem to view Nicole as a rival for Jack's affections, which was something that Nicole had been worried about. Instead, she seemed thrilled to have a permanent adult female in her life.

Nicole recalled a conversation they'd had with the therapist a month before the wedding. She had expressed her concerns to the man over the phone before they all had met in person.

"Chloe, do you understand that once your uncle and Nicole get married, she'll be moving in to the house with you?" His gentle voice was calm, but Jack's hand had tightened on hers.

Glancing his way, she saw him fighting not to frown. She held her breath while she waited for the answer.

Chloe shrugged. "Yeah, I guess."

What did that mean?

"Are you okay with this?"

Chloe's large blue eyes widened. "Yeah. It will be fun."

Fun?

"She'd be like a mother to you, like your uncle Jack is a father."

At that time, Nicole wanted him to stop pressing. If Chloe was fine with it, she didn't want to change her mind.

Chloe frowned, and her heart sank. "My mommy left me alone a lot. Does this mean I'll be alone again?"

She could no longer sit in her chair. Nicole jumped from her seat and knelt in front of the child. Taking the child's hands in hers, she made her a promise. "We will not leave you alone, Chloe. Jack and I will love you and take care of you, and you will never be alone in our home."

The child glanced from Nicole to Jack and back again. "That's fine, then."

And it had been settled.

Nicole roused from her memory as Jack spun the wheel expertly and pulled into a vacant lot they'd looked at eight months ago.

Or it had been a vacant lot. Where nothing had been previously, the ranch house she'd told him she always wanted to live in sat in quiet splendor. She sucked in a deep breath, stunned.

"Jack Quinn, what did you do?" She forced her voice through her emotion-constricted throat.

"I listened." He turned to face her. "You wanted roots. A place to raise a family. And you wanted a husband who would never lie to you or betray you. Well, I've already given you the last part."

She nodded. Jack had asked her before they married if she'd mind if he switched careers. He didn't like that his job would sometimes require him to hide the truth from his family. He had accepted an offer and now worked in a corporate security office less than an hour from Sutter Springs. She'd been worried about his job satisfaction, but he loved his new career. And he loved coming home to her and Chloe each night.

"You told me to use the settlement from Beverly's case on something I wanted. I wanted to build you the house you wanted, so we could have the room to raise the horses we talked about and we would have a place to raise our children."

"Are you getting rid of me?"

They both looked at Chloe's pinched little face. Nicole reached over and smoothed a loving hand down the child's pale face. "No, love, you are our first child. And always will be."

"That's right." Jack smiled at her, then opened his door. "Let's go and explore, shall we?"

She could barely wait to see what was inside the house. She and Chloe exited the car. When she took Chloe's right hand, Jack held out his own and held the left one. Together, the trio entered the house through the Florida room, a large, enclosed porch off the main house. Through there, they entered a large kitchen.

It was perfect. There were four bedrooms and a finished basement. The dining room overlooked a large wooden deck that ran the length of the back of the house. From the sliding glass doors, she could see a spacious yard with a pond near the far end.

"Jack, it's just like I always imagined." Tears stung her eyes. She blinked them back. He was right. He'd listened to every word she'd said about the home she wanted to have one day.

Chloe was bouncing up and down. "Can I see my room, Uncle Jack? Can I, please?"

Grinning, he tugged both his girls along the hall to the two back bedrooms. "This is yours, Chloe."

She ran into the room, squealing at the pink-and-green-decorated room.

"Joyce helped."

As Chloe ran about inspecting every corner, Nicole drew closer to Jack and slid her arm around his waist. When his arm settled across her shoulders, she sighed, content.

"When should we tell her?" Jack whispered into her ear, his breath warm on her face.

"Let's do it now."

He nodded. "Hey, Chloe, Nicole and I have something to tell you."

Alarmed, Chloe stopped and whirled around, her gaze bouncing between them.

"It's nothing bad, honey." Jack beckoned her to come closer.

She did, her steps cautious. Nicole's heart felt battered by her wariness.

"What is it?"

Nicole took over the discussion. "Sweetie, now that your uncle and I are married, the three of us are a family. So, remember how we told you in the car that you would always be our first kid?"

"Yeah."

Jack tussled her hair. "We want to make it official. How would you feel if Nicole and I adopted you?"

Chloe's eyes grew huge. "Adopted? You mean, you'd be my mom and dad?"

They both nodded and waited.

It didn't take long for her to decide. She rushed at them with a shriek, hugging them both. By the time she settled down, tears were in all their eyes.

"When can we do that? Can I call you Mom and Dad? Will I get brothers and sisters?"

Nicole wiped her wet cheeks dry and laughed. "We started the process already. So, very soon you will be our daughter. And yes, I'd love it if you called us Mom and Dad."

"I hope you'll have sisters and brothers someday," Jack added. "But we'll leave that up to God."

An hour later, they locked the house up and headed back to the car. Nicole couldn't wait to begin decorating their home and moving in. Her heart was full. God had given her everything she'd been so afraid to ask for.

That night, after an exhausted Chloe had gone to bed, she joined her husband in the kitchen of their apartment. He turned when she placed a soft hand on his shoulder and pulled her into his embrace.

"I love you so much, Jack. Thank you for not giving up on me."

He leaned down and brushed his lips against hers. She shivered. "I love you, too. I will spend the rest of my days showing you just how much."

His lips captured hers again, telling her without words that his heart belonged to her completely.

* * * * *

*If you enjoyed this book, don't miss the other
heart-stopping Amish adventures from
Dana R. Lynn's Amish Country Justice series:*

*Available now from Love Inspired Suspense!
Find more great reads at www.LoveInspired.com.*

Dear Reader,

Sometimes when I write, I include a character in a book, never expecting that I will grow to love that fictional person so much that he or she will need their own story. One such character for me was Sergeant Nicole Dawson.

Nicole first entered the scene in *Amish Country Threats*. She was a secondary character, and honestly, in my rough draft, she didn't even have a name. By the end of the story, though, she was beginning to intrigue me.

So did Special Agent Jack Quinn, who didn't get his first name until his second appearance in *Amish Christmas Escape*. The interactions between these two made me wonder what had gone wrong between them. And how I could get them back together!

I hope you enjoyed reading *Amish Cradle Conspiracy*. I would love to hear from you! I can be reached at www.danarlynn.com. Or find me on Facebook and Instagram.

Blessings!
Dana R. Lynn

LOVE INSPIRED

Stories to uplift and inspire

Fall in love with Love Inspired—
inspirational and uplifting stories of faith
and hope. Find strength and comfort in
the bonds of friendship and community.
Revel in the warmth of possibility and the
promise of new beginnings.

Sign up for the Love Inspired newsletter
at **LoveInspired.com** to be the first
to find out about upcoming titles,
special promotions and exclusive content.

CONNECT WITH US AT:

f Facebook.com/LoveInspiredBooks

Twitter.com/LoveInspiredBks

COMING NEXT MONTH FROM
Love Inspired Suspense

UNDERCOVER ASSIGNMENT
Rocky Mountain K-9 Unit • by Dana Mentink
Innkeeper and single father Sam Kavanaugh suspects someone is after his three-year-old son—so K-9 officer Daniella Vargas goes undercover as the little boy's nanny with her protection dog, Zara. But can they solve the case and its mysterious connection to Sam's late wife before it's too late?

COLD CASE KILLER PROFILE
Quantico Profilers • by Jessica R. Patch
Searching for the perfect morning landscape to paint leads forensic artist Brigitte Linsey straight to a dead body—and a narrow escape from the Sunrise Serial Killer still on the scene. Now that she's the killer's number one target, partnering with FBI special agent Duke Jericho might be her only chance at surviving...

FATAL FORENSIC INVESTIGATION
by Darlene L. Turner
While interviewing the Coastline Strangler's only surviving victim, forensic artist Scarlet Wells is attacked and left with amnesia. Now she's his next mark and has no choice but to work with constable Jace Allen to hunt down the killer before he strikes again...

RANCH UNDER SIEGE
by Sommer Smith
Boston-based journalist Madison Burke has two goals when she heads to the Oklahoma ranch where her father works as a foreman: heal a family rift...and escape the person targeting her. But when danger follows her, can Madison rely on ranch owner and former navy SEAL Briggs Thorpe to keep her alive?

HUNTED IN THE WILDERNESS
by Kellie VanHorn
Framed for murder and corporate espionage, future aerotech company CEO Haley Whitcombe flees in her plane with evidence that could clear her name—and is shot out of the sky. Now trapped in North Cascades National Park, she must work with park ranger Ezra Dalton to survive the wilderness and assassins.

VANISHED WITHOUT A TRACE
by Sarah Hamaker
Assistant district attorney Henderson Parker just wants to follow the lead in Twin Oaks, Virginia, to find his missing sister—not team up with podcaster Elle Updike. But after mysterious thugs make multiple attacks on his life, trusting Elle and her information might be his best opportunity to save them all...

LOOK FOR THESE AND OTHER LOVE INSPIRED BOOKS WHEREVER BOOKS ARE SOLD, INCLUDING MOST BOOKSTORES, SUPERMARKETS, DISCOUNT STORES AND DRUGSTORES.

LISCNM0522

Get 4 FREE REWARDS!

We'll send you 2 FREE Books plus 2 FREE Mystery Gifts.

FREE Value Over **$20**

Both the **Love Inspired®** and **Love Inspired® Suspense** series feature compelling novels filled with inspirational romance, faith, forgiveness, and hope.

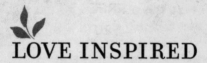